girl #3

girl #3

Nichole McGill

KEY PORTER BOOKS

Copyright © 2009 by Nichole McGill

Library and Archives Canada Cataloguing in Publication

McGill, Nichole
    Girl #3 / Nichole McGill.

ISBN 978-1-55470-143-8

I. Title. II. Title: Girl number three.

PS8575.G443G57 2009   jC813'.6   C2008-906956-0

The publisher gratefully acknowledges the support of the Canada Council for the Arts and the Ontario Arts Council for its publishing program. We acknowledge the support of the Government of Ontario through the Ontario Media Development Corporation's Ontario Book Initiative.

We acknowledge the financial support of the Government of Canada through the Book Publishing Industry Development Program (BPIDP) for our publishing activities.

Key Porter Books Limited
Six Adelaide Street East, Tenth Floor
Toronto, Ontario
Canada M5C 1H6

www.keyporter.com

Text design: Marijke Friesen
Electronic formatting: Alison Carr

Printed and bound in Canada

09 10 11 12 13 5 4 3 2 1

For John, who never doubted

1

waiting

#1
the girls

The reason I may die today is because I saw Girl #2 last fall.

I'm not superstitious or anything. And don't think I scare easily, either. I've dealt with plenty of creeps before—at school dances, on the TTC, on forbidden joyrides downtown with Alicia, on the street. You know—guys that stare at you until their brains fall out of their mouths. I may only be fourteen, but I've handled them before. I may be, like, five foot nothing, with stubby legs, but when I run in a track meet or circle the rectangular military grid of suburban houses that mark my "hood," I surprise everyone.

Still, I know in my skin that all the wrong things that have happened in the five months from then until now—the sightings, the blue car, the other cars that would follow—they all started with that stupid gorgeous Indian summer afternoon in October, when I took Ripley for a bike ride through my ravine.

What else was I supposed to do? It was after

school. I didn't have track for the first time in forever. Alicia (best friend and fellow track fiend and Jaguar team mate) had skipped out on geography to grab a bus to Sherway Gardens to "catch the sidewalk sales" with Melissa (a supposed hurdler whose smile is as tight as her pants). And all because:

"Her cousin works at lulu's, Syd, she can get me a discount," she said, eyes pleading.

Later, Alicia complained about the state of her current yoga pants for hours, barely slipping in a muttered apology to me—I don't know if it was for ditching me or being friends with Skank Butt, who was a lazy inch away from being kicked off the track team anyway. Whatever, girlfriend.

Anyway, that was Alicia. Mum was at work . . . naturally. Thursday meant the late shift at The Boutique in the Kingsway, squeezing super skinny mums with bleached teeth into overpriced jeans and silk-screened T-shirts from Italy.

So it was just me that day. And as I walked the one block from school to home, attempting to not mentally chew out Alicia for going shopping with Bimbo-Girl, the near-tropical air stole in through the bottoms of my roomy stretch pants and stroked the backs of my knees. If the fibres in my legs hadn't been screaming murder at me all day, I would've gone for a run, even on my track day off. But thanks to an excessive training regiment courtesy of Coach "Unibrow" Bremner, my muscles were finding new ways to detach themselves from my shin bone to avoid further punishment.

And there she was: Ripley. Waiting patiently for me at home, chained to a rusty pipe in the garage. The first fallen leaves had inched their way in and nestled in her spokes. Ripley's my tough-girl mountain bike and she's like this garish neon-orange colour, her frame plastered with crazy purple stickers, half of which have ripped off, leaving sticky grey ghosts. I so love her, and not just because her clashing colours continue to offend my every-hair-glued-in-the-right-place mother. I found Ripley beaten up and abandoned behind the local strip mall. When I dragged her mud-splattered skeleton home, Mum immediately turned her nose up at her *dreadful* state of hygiene. I was forced to resort to a paper route and Dad money to get her fixed up. Ripley and I are blood, even if she is mostly metal and rubber.

So I returned her shiny grin and took her up on her challenge. I unlocked her and pointed her knobbed tires down my quiet side street, cruised past all the two-storey houses dappled with sun, and emerged into the smoky chaos and traffic on the bottleneck that is Eglinton Avenue. Luckily, there's a sliver of bike path for little old me. If I looked up and to the right from my fuzzy handlebars, I would see a wall of exhaust from cars spinning in the air where three—count 'em, three—major highways meet. Add to that the jets from the airport circling above the polluted mass. Who wants to see that?

So I choked back exhaust as I whipped by seven lanes of cars frozen in rush hour (suckers!), gaining crazy momentum as the path ran downhill, then suddenly dipped to the left and—relief!—Ripley and I shot under a canopy of trees that were just turning into flames. I was in and flying through a protective tunnel of green, red, and orange. I sped past fat bushes and hairy maples, picking up colossal speed. The wind was pushing my short black hair so it stood on end and probably looked whacked (yeah, yeah—no helmet. I *know*, Mum, Officer Murdoch-who-came-to-speak-at-our-high-school), but I didn't care. This was my place. It was my ravine. Here, I didn't have to worry about Alicia hanging with Melissa, or accusing me of liking the guys she likes, or that she's already moving up the popular ranks at Parkside C.I. despite being a niner while I kind of stay on the periphery, or that I hadn't heard from Dad since last Christmas and why couldn't Parkside have a mountain biking team? All of these thoughts dissolved and flew away with the wind. I whipped past my favourite part, the bushy forest that climbs the hill to the quiet street above. The trees are a wall between the forest and plains except where they cut in an upside down "U" to reveal a dirt path that winds up the hill.

And that's where and when I saw her: Girl #2.

I know what you're going to say, "Wait, there's no way this could have happened in October! You mean, August, maybe beginning of September, right?"

Nope. I saw her on October the fifteenth, a Wednesday. And I fully realize the implications. Like I said, I don't scare easily. Not that there was anything immediately eerie about her appearance in my ravine—apart from, you know, the obvious.

When I zipped past her, my eyes took a snapshot in full detail that still causes my eyeballs to ache in memory. Girl #2 was perched in a maple tree set just a little back from the path entrance and so spindly there was no way it could have actually held her weight, even if she did weigh nothing. Her thin legs dangled and swayed with the wind, her auburn hair straight and serious, cut with Cleopatra bangs. Her eyes, leaf green, caught in the sun, piercing in a flash, the leaves around her turning into flames.

Of course, I knew in my gut who she was immediately. Everybody knows what Girl #2 looks like—everyone in Toronto, anyway.

But it gets weirder. I not only saw her, I *felt* her: just as surely as if she had laid a thin, white hand on my head. I felt a tingling on my scalp and a current cut through my skin that launched me past the forest and around the bend to the dead-grass plateau where the kids' swings are, their metal chains tangled and rusting together. It was only there that I dared set my sneakers on the ground and look back to double-check, my heart searing my skin.

Alright, maybe she did freak me out a bit.

I can't say how long I stood there waiting for my

skin to settle. It's not like I had to be home for dinner:
Mum wouldn't be home until after 9:30 p.m.—the
curve of her perfectly painted-on eyebrows mirrored in
dark bags under each eye. She'd walk in the door and
brew a black tea that she'd leave around the house in
a half-empty gold-dipped teacup that had been passed
down from a dead but friendly great aunt.

Until then, I had plenty of dead time to fall into
and so that's exactly what I did. I stood there on the
bike path watching as a couple of other bikers (obviously just recreational) cruised past, lolling their
heads, barely beating walkers, completely oblivious to
the fact that the most famous, the most known girl in
Toronto at that moment was scrutinizing them from
the safety of her shelter barely ten metres away; that is,
if she was still there. I couldn't see her from this angle.

You have to go back.

This was what my Super Bossy Voice said. She's
like this demanding, brassy voice inside my head—
kind of like a know-it-all older sister who always gets
grounded for setting the neighbour's petunia bed on
fire or baiting a supermodel-wannabe to a slugfest.
Maybe you have a crazy voice in your head, too, one
that says all of the things you're thinking but are too
scared to *admit* you're thinking, much less say out
loud.

So I said back to her, silently: No freaking way!

*It's okay. I mean, what could she possibly do to
you in her state?*

She couldn't do anything to me. Girl #2 was just a girl—like me. Actually, when I thought about it—frozen on the pathway, staring at the black smudge on my sneakers, a sudden warm gust tickling the blond hairs on my neck, then the black spikes of my shorn hair—I calmed down. Girl #2 was a lot like me, right? But not in the obvious ways.

She had long hair, for one, fine like red thread. She was tall—taller than me anyway, but that's not exactly difficult. And she lived downtown, amidst a million tiny shops and corner stores bursting with flowers and fruit and life. Not like me, in west end snor-burbia. I had to bike two clicks to the nearest strip mall for an average chocolate bar.

Still, neither of us had siblings, and our birthdays were a month apart. She also liked completely obnoxious mixtures of colours like lime green with chocolate and orange. And the place that she'd escape to when she was most upset—and the papers went on and on about this as if she'd asked for it or something—was her ravine.

I should probably explain the ravines. Toronto's basically a slab of concrete except for four green ravines that break it up, and each of these ravines has a thin, drizzling river in it. There's mine—quiet Mimico in the far west—then there's the Humber, which has a fancy old mill in it. In the east (Scarborough) there's the Rouge, which is also boring, but at least it can boast having deer. At least, that's the rumour. And right in the middle there's the Don; it has a river that belches fish farts into the air and a highway running through it, as well as enough dense forest surrounding it that a girl could find her own private hideaway. And Girl #2 had done just that. Hers was a simple platform in a beautiful birch tree.

Still, there was one major thing that set us apart. Girl #2 is dead.

I craned my neck to look back. The path was empty. With shuffling legs, I turned Ripley around. I had to see if this girl—who had been buried four days earlier, on Sunday, October 11, in a private ceremony that spilled out into the streets, who was on the front page of the papers since she went missing in early September—if she really was hanging out, sitting on a tree branch, in my ravine.

I biked back. I churned each leg slowly, feeling my heart beating about a hundred miles a minute with each turn of my leg, until I reached the tree canopy where she had been swaying and looked up.

Only the leaves blinked back.

It took me a while to register this. No way! She *had* been there. I had felt her.

I dismounted Ripley and walked up the grassy hill trying to catch a glimpse. Ripley's knobbly tires chewed up the grass as I trudged, but I still couldn't see her.

My heart was no longer beating superstitious panic—now I was frustrated. I ran up the rest of the hill, digging in my sneakers, grass and dirt kicking backward as I went up the rough path, thick bushes to either side of me. I reached the top only to see a thin alley of green between two high backyard fences.

No one.

But I *did* see her on the fifteenth of October, exactly five months ago, in my ravine—piddly Mimico, it's not even a real river, barely a drizzle of a creek—two valleys west of the wild downtown ravine where a week earlier, a man walking his dog found her wrapped on that platform she'd made in the white arms of her birch tree.

Nothing can convince me otherwise.

So it's no surprise I guess, that it's her I'm thinking of right this very moment. It's March now. Winter came but it hasn't quite checked out, as the piles of snotty snow around my sneakers prove.

Can you feel that?

A wind like an iced hand is inching up my spine. I'm in my ravine, wimpy Mimico, crouching in a bed of dead, mulched leaves. My skin puckers into goose bumps, my trembling thigh muscles on the verge of seizing from crouching too long in the same position. Only the adrenaline, the sweet adrenaline coursing from behind my bulged eyes to my chilled feet reminds me that I'm *alive*, so terrifyingly *alive* even as I strain not to move.

My brain is screaming. Can you hear it?

If you move, he might see you! And if he sees you,

he'll collect you . . . and if he collects you, you may never see anything ever again.

The wind knocks on my nose but I'm not going to answer. I command my muscles to stay put.

I won't let him catch me. I won't become Girl #3.

#2
nothing happens in etobicoke

Nothing ever happens in Etobicoke. Or at least it didn't use to. But that chance sighting of Girl #2 five months ago changed everything and now, here I am, crouched and frozen behind a bush ...

Maybe I should have stayed in last night in typical Etobicoke fashion? It was after dinner—at least, *I* showed up to the table. Mum hadn't returned from a salon appointment so I went ahead and made myself a bowl of angel hair pasta with loads of butter and parmesan. Afterwards, I lazed on the leather couch in the living room, nestled under an embroidered throw with a metal bowl filled with buttery popcorn balanced between my knees. In the DVD player was a copy of my favourite movie: *Without Limits*.

You mean, it's on your top ten, too?! That's okay—no one else has heard of it either. It's about this American track star in the seventies who ran some of the distances I do—the 1,500-, the 3,000-metres—and when he raced, he ignored all advice to pace himself:

he ran until he had nothing left in the tank, until his knees buckled and the sacs in his lungs ached. He ran each race like his life depended on it.

If I ran that way, Coach Unibrow would berate me until I picked myself up from the pink rocks of our shabby track and did another lap, to serve me right for doing something that dumb and to deter me from ever doing it again. I was dreaming of happier times with my middle school coach, nurturing Ms. Cavanaugh, when Mum announced her presence with a shrill:

"Is *this* how you're going to spend the evening?"

I jumped. The metal bowl of popcorn slid down my knees but I caught it before chaos ensued. Mum was on high octane. I had conveniently forgotten to remember that Sunday was the Peterson Wedding, tomorrow, the dress rehearsal, and we had to look our best since the Petersons were not only once-removed family, they were capital-R Rich. We, I, had to be perfect.

Mum had taken the day off work for a lengthy salon appointment, where she got some serious work done. Any signs of grey in her raven hair had been annihilated; her face was exfoliated, pumped up, and whatever other voodoo magic those women in white doctor coats with thick Eastern European accents work on women who want to look perfect.

The black bags under Mum's eyes now shone like eerie revitalized half-moons, her hair was as black as Snow White's mane. She was stunning, but Mum has always been beautiful. To me, she's like a forties film star who's walked off the black-and-white screen to reach for a tube of crimson lipstick. Only real life has made her weary and she's constantly searching for the lit cigarette she left in the last frame.

"Well . . . ?!"

I stretched out my right leg until my knee popped. Ouch! Mental note: Gotta run on people's lawns instead of the sidewalk. If I was a guy, I would have scratched my crotch in apathy. Considering Mum's state, if I'd done *that*, she would have blown, taking out her, me, the kitchen, and my popcorn all at once.

"Tell me your bridesmaid dress is still pressed and hanging up in your closet?"

Yes, I'm one of the bridesmaids for this wedding. Oh joy. Check that—*junior* bridesmaid for a cousin I *used* to only see at odd Christmases. And then Dad left.

Heavy sigh: "I haven't touched the dress since you bought it."

Forced it upon me, I wanted to say, enslaved me with it. A month ago, when the colour swatches arrived in the mail, Mum had marched me to the seamstress on Avenue Road where I was measured, pinched, bound, analyzed—my petite frame, my "unusually muscular bottom" and my non-existent chest a great source of discussion among the ladies who were forced to alter the main design. I was humiliated, basically.

"So," continued Mum, "does that mean it's hanging up, or balled in a pile at the bottom of your closet with everything else?" Her eyes pulsated with madness. "I was just up there, Syd, and I didn't see it."

Wow, I thought. If she's calling me "Syd" instead of my over-flowery given name—"Sidonia"—then she is really primed to blow and she needs no help from me. I had to be very adult here. I had to silence the screams from Super Bossy Voice: *She's snooping in your closet?!* So I enunciated very clearly to make sure she understood:

"It's . . . han-ging . . . UP! I haven't touched it. Why would I touch it?"

Why would I wear it?

This seemed to bring Mum down to about a level-three degree of anxiety, which still meant she was two levels above normal.

"Please check on it for me. I want to see it," she pleaded again, no doubt embarrassed to have a daughter like me.

Unbelievable. I had to run upstairs to check on a *dress* to calm down my mother. I'm sure this is why I'm an only child. Can you imagine if I had to check in on something living, like a sibling?

I placed my rescued popcorn bowl on the table, tossed the throw aside and silently brushed past Mum, whom I mirror in height, near-black hair, pale skin, and dollar-sized brown eyes—but that's about it.

"The throw is for the couch, Sidonia," Mum muttered as I marched down the hall.

Since couches get cold and need comfort, didn't

you know? In reality, the throw was to cover tears in the leather that we couldn't afford to fix. Since I prefer the roof attached to our house rather than blown off it, I knew better than to mention this fact aloud. In fact, there's a lot I can't say aloud: Adults really aren't equipped to hear the truth, especially when it comes from a fourteen-year-old. So why rock the boat?

My socked feet padded up the stairs and turned left into the north side of the attic that is my bedroom. I actually like my room, even though some girls I know have closets this size. I used to. But this new-ish bedroom has slanted ceilings that are kind of cool and are choice for putting up posters.

As I reached for the closet door, my shoulders hunched in horror. What if the dress was bunched at the bottom of my closet? What if it was lost? I hadn't seen it since we brought it home in its bland nude bag. I couldn't even picture what the bag looked like. Horror was replaced with spreading, tingly elation. I had an out! Tonight and tomorrow, I could fake the stomach flu, guzzle castor oil, and pull a bulimic fit in the bathroom. I'd be prostrate over a toilet bowl explaining to a revolted Mum in between gags and spitting (how unladylike) that the dress was *lost*! Even if I wasn't puking my guts out (as if Mum could handle *that*), there was no possible way I could play junior bridesmaid in "pale peach with azure beading." I was missing the costume.

It was a nice fantasy. Of course, the dress bag *was*

in my closet, hanging bone straight like it had for two months, defiant in a sea of yoga tops, practical pants, and track gear. It comes with a blazing blue-beaded purse that reminds me of a Hello Kitty purse I treasured when I was two—then I got over it.

I would have been bummed out all evening if the doorbell hadn't rung just then and Alicia's singsong voice hadn't travelled up the stairs, buoying my spirits.

"Hello, Mrs. Johansen. Is Syd in?"

Alicia was supposed to be grounded, which meant that she had either struck a hard bargain with her über-strict pastor-dad, Father Solomon (not likely). Or she had scrambled out the window of her basement bedroom, hopped the hedge, and ran the four blocks to my house, and, in typical Alicia fashion, had not secreted a drop of sweat in the process. I felt a glimmer of hope. Maybe she was looking to make up after our most recent friendship fracture—her blaming me for getting grounded last week? Maybe I was going to get a much deserved apology?

Alicia scurried up to my room with a warm smile, but not before Mum chimed in a perky voice that was too brittle to be real, "Not too late, Sidonia. Tonight, it's an *early* night."

"What's your mum on?" whispered Alicia after I had safely closed the door and turned up the speakers attached to my measly MP3 player.

"Are you kidding me? The *wedding*?" I answered.

"What wedding?"

Now Alicia's supposed to be my best friend, well until lately—my only good female friend who I can supposedly share everything with—but she has this annoying habit of instantly forgetting any of the rare problems that I share with her, like, twice a year, choosing to focus instead on the hundreds of minor crises she goes through in a week. But what could I say? I couldn't stay mad at Alicia. She's never bad-mouthed me, she cheers me on at track meets, and she's never stuck her tongue down the throat of a guy after I said I liked him. I mean, I could never tell her that I saw Girl #2 in our ravine or even bring up Girl #1 (who Alicia went to school with before she transferred to Parkside) but as friends go, she rated pretty high.

I ignored the fact that Alicia was dressed for business: low-rider stretch pants, crop top, subtle glitter painting her cheekbones, and Jeri curls that spiralled over her forehead. I had a feeling I knew what she was going to ask. So I threw her a curve ball.

"Mum thinks my Dad's going to show at the wedding," I said apathetically.

Alicia's caramel eyes popped. "Seriously?!"

I have no idea why I let this spill—maybe I was testing Alicia, maybe I really believed it. Maybe I had picked up the phone two days ago and overheard a nervous Mum nonchalantly asking The Bride if a certain ex-husband was anticipated to show.

"God, no, Clare—it's not like he's blood!" said The Bride in her typical huff-and-puff manner. "And what with all the problems at the border these days, I'm surprised if he could get in." Then she muttered, "Unless *Duncan* invited him."

So there was a slim chance that my senile great-uncle Duncan, king of the dysfunctional Forest Hill and Parkside Petersons, had decided to piss off everyone and invite the charming ex-husband of his shunned great niece to the wedding of his favourite one. Nice. Great.

I couldn't breathe.

This tends to happen when I think I'm really going to see Dad again and now I had a suddenly seriously concerned Alicia asking me a million questions while I hyperventilated on my comforter:

"Is he really? God, what are you going to do? Is your Mum going to burn his clothes in a bonfire again (and get another warning from the police)? What are you going to wear to the wedding? Is it pretty? Why are your eyes bugging out?"

It took me a while to get a grip—maybe to Alicia it was only a few minutes, but when I'm in paralyzed mode, time inches by painfully. Thanks Mum—I guess I get the "frozen squirrel in the headlights" thing from her, too.

Exhale; inhale, Syd. It's real simple, girl. Let's just do it: exhale . . . inhale . . . exhale . . .

I honked out some air, started choking, then muttered a "probably not going to happen—don't want to talk about it," which killed that line of questioning, thank God. With a relieved smile, Alicia started in on what she came over to talk about in the first place:

"You have to get me into the dance tonight! You'll never guess who's coming!"

I already knew. That's right: the one, the only, the coolest track star in Etobicoke—R.S.—was going to show at our stupid dance tonight. I didn't listen to the girl gossip, what a waste of time, but this time . . . okay—my heart flipped at the thought of R.S. He was in grade eleven, blond, tall, whatever, and a guy so cool, he broke sprint records with a shrug of his shoulder. And I really liked him because he shrugged off skanky track bunnies just as easily.

Alicia was still going on and on. She'd told her dad that she needed to come to my house to study for a big test and he'd let her out of her grounding. She had to be back by eleven, which gave us *just* enough time. See, *I* needed to help Alicia go to the dance. *I* needed to go with her and if her dad called my mum, on a rampage, then my mum, who probably wouldn't even notice we'd snuck out because we'd leave my door closed and the radio *just* loud enough, would corroborate our story. She topped this description of her elaborate plan off with this corker, narrowing her eyes:

"I mean, don't you think you owe me one?"

It was a desperate plan from a desperate friend who knew I didn't do school dances, and knew very well what happened the last time we went. I shivered as the faces of creepy guys (one face in particular) rose

in my mind. Forget it: school dances were for skanks
and alcoholics-in-training. But Alicia kept nattering *on*
as if she didn't know this about me. It didn't help that
I replaced her face with a picture of me coming face-to-
face with Dad and the Second Wife, whom I still had
never seen. I would be wearing my horrific peach junior bridesmaid dress with "azure" beads sparkling on
my flat chest. This time I made sure to breathe. The
details of Alicia's hysterical plan faded into the background as I practised inhaling and exhaling.

Good training for right now, too, in my place in
the bush. I have to breathe. If I don't breathe, I'll pass
out. If I pass out, it's game over.

#3
this morning

Where did things go so wrong?

The game plan for me this morning was easy: Get up at 6 a.m., do my papers, be home by eight, eight thirty *latest* to get all dolled up by Mum, and get to the church in time for rehearsal at ten thirty. Super easy, right?

I didn't get up right away. It probably had to do with going to bed way past midnight, kept awake by a new awareness that my only taboo fantasy could become flesh. And it was cold, the nighttime air whispering its message on the streets through the crack in my window: *Winter ain't gone, not by a long shot.* So much for The Bride's hope for a flowery, spring wedding. And cold makes me want to cocoon.

Add to that I'd been having anxiety attacks that kept me up for most of the night—and there went my beauty sleep.

Don't think about Dad. Don't picture him. He ain't gonna show this weekend! And don't picture yourself in the Dress!

I repeated these lines as I watched the quilt rise and fall over my face with every breath balmy against my cheeks. Under this safe cover, I was snug in a womb. It was easy to ignore my alarm shrieking every ten minutes. I did a quick calculation: Only twenty-four more alarms to ignore and I'd miss the rehearsal completely and maybe be ejected from the wedding party! I could stay under that quilt all day and day-dream about someone. But Mum was awake and on my case.

On an ordinary day, Mum isn't up before seven thirty. After that she grunts like a groggy gorilla until her morning bunch of bananas has been placed in front of her—or, in her case, her cup of coffee. I'm the one who gets breakfast going, brings in the morning paper, puts on the java, and lets the aroma drift up the stairs to do its wake-up work.

Except for this morning. This morning, after the third snooze alarm at six thirty, Mum marched into my bedroom and, with a snap of her thin arm, ripped the quilt cover off me. I flinched as the cold air splashed over my face and bare arms.

"Whaddaya doing?!" I squawked, shielding my body like I was naked.

"We have only four hours to get ready," she said curtly in her new robotic morning voice. Then she turned on her elegant heel and marched out into the bathroom where she promptly turned on the shower.

Four *hours?* Four minutes is time enough to pull a

dress over my head, thanks. After this stupid wedding, I better get the old Half-Crazy Mum back. If the new one stays, she's going to send us both into therapy.

I grasped for my "uniform," the one waiting patiently for me on my dresser: Black Adidas track pants and a black T-shirt topped by a red K-way with permanent black newsprint smeared under the right arm. I tucked all my hair under a black baseball cap (the logo of one of Dad's companies ripped off) that perfectly shields my round-pebble eyes. You might not even guess I'm female in this get-up—it drives Mum mental, which is why I scurried down the stairs, shoved a muffin into my pocket, grabbed my sneakers, and bolted out the door before new Robot Mum could confront me again. Although she tried—soaking wet and in a towel and coming halfway down the stairs, all the while lecturing me on the dangers of the newsprint that I, inevitably, would get all over my soon-to-be-peach polished fingernails.

I raced into the garage and unlocked Ripley from her hitch at the gas pipe, grabbed my folded-up rattling metal cart (another ravine find), slung it over my shoulders and glided down the driveway and into the street.

Early-morning fog wrapped like grey fleece around me, and the cold air licked my cheeks. Every house I passed was blurry behind a fog curtain. The sun was still asleep.

"You gotta get me there, girl," I whispered to

Ripley. "Don't let me end up in a ditch." There are no sidewalks here—the road rolls off into ditches where there are scattered patches of leftover ice. The wires on the giant hydro towers crackled above us. My stomach grumbled for the muffin in my pocket but it was also doing flip-flops of dread. Maybe I could keep biking forever, all the way to downtown. I did it once, until my thigh muscles burned.

I don't know why I like my paper route so much. It's not like I deliver *real* newspapers. When Dad was a boy, he got to deliver major newspapers like *The Star* and *The Globe and Mail*.

He says he remembers all the important stories from those days: The October Crisis, the year that the Canadians beat the Russians in hockey (only they were called the Soviets then). He knew them all. But they don't let kids deliver those papers anymore— maybe they're afraid of them reading or something— so I'm left with *The Islington Carrier: Etobicoke's Oldest Community Newspaper*. The front page of *The Carrier* runs pictures of puppies or seniors or kids wearing ice cream. If it's a big news day, they run all three.

Still, this route is mine and so is the money; not that I'd brag about the amount. Plus, I'm the best carrier my manager, Gord-O, has. On Ripley, I can do sixty-two houses in twenty-five minutes flat and he knows it. Sometimes on Saturday mornings, Gord-O hangs around, idling in his green minivan until I pick up the papers from my drop-off on Main Street. He offers me a doughnut ball from the mega pack he buys every morning. He's okay.

I turned onto Main. Ahead I saw a grey lump that resembled papers thrown outside the bus shelter and, directly across from the shelter, there was a car idling on the side of road. For a second, I thought it was roly poly Gord-O waiting with a box of greasy doughnuts and burnt coffee. Except, like I said, he drives that green minivan with *The Carrier* logo on it and as I biked closer, I saw that the *vehicle* (that's really the proper way to describe these things), the *vehicle* was a car and it was dark blue.

Weird. Main is, like, a narrow country road. There's no room to park on it without blocking the main lanes of traffic. Sure, at this time of the morning, traffic is nil, but still—weird.

When I got to the drop-off, I saw that I had extra gaudy promo flyers to insert into each of my sixty-two *Carrier* papers. I groaned. Usually Gord-O warns me, today he hadn't. I leaned Ripley against the shelter, dug a thumbnail into the ends of the flat cord that holds the papers together, and thumbed each *Carrier* copy as I counted. I was also short two papers. If he screws up the paper count and he's hung around, Gord-O gives me three doughnut holes and a goofy shrug. Adults can be so unreliable.

I loathe the flyers, but I still do a good job. I slide in the slippery inserts with their spines nestled in the exact middle of the paper. You'd never know they were separate parts the way I do it. All the while I kept my eye on the blue car that was idling right across from me behind a curtain of dissipating fog. Mentally, I prepared my description for the police:

"No, officer, I didn't look at the licence plate number or note the make of car or anything. It wasn't a Jeep or a BMW or a fancy anything—it was a crappy, I mean *nondescript*, dark blue car that looked like a thousand other crappy plastic cars. It disappeared into the fog and its windows were black smoked glass."

I continued to ignore it, opened another *Carrier*, slid another flyer in—*slip-slap*, *slip-slap*. I still kept an eye on the car. A tail of smoke plumed from its muffler.

Maybe it's one of those adult paper carriers, I thought suddenly. Remember how I said kids can't deliver real papers? These days the big papers give all the routes to men with sour faces and grumbling accents who come from Russia or Georgia or wherever and drive around in tin-can cars with bad mufflers. They hurtle rolled-up papers from their cars so they end up in flowerpots, bushes, garbage cans. They don't take the time to place the paper under a mat or put it in a mailbox. I mean, I wouldn't be happy either if that was my grown-up job but I'd sure be happier if I could deliver real papers on Ripley. Then I could read real stories while I went from house to house, maybe even share the stories I read about with Dad, the newsbug. Past tense: Could have shared stories, if he was around. I caught myself doing the not-breathing thing again—a fist closing around my lungs—and forced out some coughed air.

There! Inserts were inserted and my fingertips were already blackened. I picked up my fatter papers in their bundles and dropped them into my wire cart. Across the street, the front passenger window of the Blue Car dropped like a glass curtain. The next bundle of papers in my hand hovered over the opening of the cart, eager to meet its brothers. Through the thinning fog, I saw a shadow of a man sitting in the driver's seat. He was talking on a cell. Maybe it was to his district manager. Then I noticed a cab sign on the top of his car with the light turned off. Why hadn't I seen that before?! Because the sky was now a lighter shade of grey. The unseen fist tightened over my lungs.

Breathe, girl. It's real simple: exhale, inhale.

I remembered reading something about Girl #2 and a taxi driver. He was one of the first suspects they brought in. His face was plastered all over the front pages of the real papers that Dad used to delivered. But that was a year ago and, in the end, he wasn't the one who did it. In the end they had nothing on him that would stick.

Breathe, girl. It's real simple.

I finished loading the cart, grabbed the cool metal handle with my right hand while clutching Ripley's handlebars with my left. I walked both of these around the bus shelter to the road. Some people may find the act of biking while pulling a full cart beside you difficult, but I can do it in my sleep. Evidently. I had just swung my left leg over Ripley's crossbar and tilted the cart with my right hand, ready to take off down Pine Street toward my route, when Taxi Man spoke.

"Ex-*soose* me." Taxi Man's voice called out over the still-empty street. The driver might as well have had his thin spittle lips on my ear.

I stumbled, slapping both feet down on the pavement. The cart clattered to an upright stop. I burned my eyes into grey asphalt.

Don't look up at the guy, commanded my bossy voice. *Pretend you don't see a hand, with fingers like whitened bone, waving at you out of the corner of your eye. Just grab your cart and go.*

Except then, he called out over the empty road between us.

"Hu-LU-ow." He sounded like he was from Transylvania or something and for some reason, my muscles went numb. Transylvanian Taxi Man leaned his face forward out of the shadows. I saw a beak borrowed from an eagle and wiry eyebrows that could have, at any moment, taken flight and grabbed a rodent, soaring with it into the tall maples above us. (I wondered how that description would sound in a newspaper story.) He was also twitchy nervous, like he had just consumed fifteen coffees or a jumbo pack of apple fritters.

If Taxi Man was off-duty (and if he were a *real* taxi man), he should have been at an all-night doughnut shop by the warehouses in Rexdale, or at a greasy spoon way south, near the factories by the lake. Here in the middle there's nothing but row upon row of sleeping houses.

And me, of course.

He flicked his eyes up and down Main, licking his thin lips. He waved me to the car:

"Come here, little girl."

Did he get that line out of the basic *Creepy-Guy Handbook* or what? I gave him my best glare-stare that masked my escalating squirrel-like heart rate, planted my butt on Ripley, grasped the metal handle of my cart, cool against my palm, and biked down Pine Street, not looking back.

What a freak. I shook the chill off my shoulders, my cart rattling comfortably behind me.

The morning wind cut under my ball cap. I hit my first house, set the cart upright, reached in to pluck a paper and biked up the flat driveway right to the door.

I imagined retelling the story of Transylvanian Taxi Man to Alicia later on, except in this version, I'd say that his eyebrows really did fly off his face. ("No!" Alicia would exclaim. "Okay . . . ," I'd give in. "They just fell into his lap where they flapped like batwings!") I smirked at the brass mailbox as I placed an expertly rolled *Carrier* into its bottom rung, hearing Alicia's imagined squeals. My shoulders relaxed. I let my mind drift to the usual suspects when I did my route: the wind on my face, track, an image of R.S. crossing the finish line and catching my elated gaze on the sidelines, sharing in his victory. I headed back to my cart, a shy smile on my lips.

Transylvanian Taxi Man was now parked beside my cart facing into traffic—isn't that illegal? My cart was now within his arm's reach of the driver's window. Panic jabbed me between my shoulder blades. He hung out his open window, holding both bone-white hands up in surrender.

"I don't want to scare you, little girl. I just have to tell you something."

Now if I had brought my cellphone, I could have called Gord-O, 911, anyone. "There's a psycho taxi driver threatening my papers!" Tragically, I had a flash of just where my cell was at the moment: wedged into a crevice on the leather couch with a handful of greasy popcorn kernels. Typical for me.

"What?" I called out defiantly, my eye on my cart.

Don't you dare take my papers! my bossy voice and I threatened silently. *Even if it is only the crappy* Carrier. *These are mine, you hear?*

"Closer, closer." He flapped his hand like he was gobbling up soup.

I had no choice: He had my papers! I pedalled in slow circles down the driveway, pasting on a neutral face, trying not to stare too intensely at my cart. All Taxi Man would have to do is reach one of his freakish tree-limb arms out of the window and he'd have the handle.

Easy, girl.

"Yes," a smile broke over his crooked face.

Just a few more circles and I'd be at the car. Or so he thinks. At the last moment, I deked to the right, grabbed my cart with my left hand and pictured myself biking off down the street. Except Taxi Man did reach out one of his branch-like arms and his hand locked on my cart. I jerked to a halt on Ripley. My racing squirrel heart launched into my throat then out of my mouth.

Taxi Man lowered his voice, "I don't want to frighten you ..." (A little too late, buddy!) "But, I have this friend ..."

You have a friend—congratulations. My legs shook. I burned eyes into the metal handle of the cart, willing it to move. I test Taxi Man's grip with a gentle pull—some give, but not enough.

"My friend, he likes little girls. Little girls like you."

Now I'm freaked. It was like I had been sweating and, with those words, Taxi Man poured a bucket of ice water down my spine. The picture on top of my cart filled my blurry vision: I knew this girl—four-year-old Beatrice Smith, who lived on our street. On the front page of *The Carrier*, she was attempting to eat blueberry pie at a charity event. I jerked at the cart once more—no give.

Look at him!

I forced myself to turn my head toward Taxi Man, tried to commit all the features of his face to memory just like the picture of little Beatrice was now permanently imprinted into my brain. But it was like my muscles filled with sluggish ice and I could only lift my eyes, straining against my eyelids.

Taxi Man whispered across the short void that now separated us. His face was filled with fatherly concern. His words magnified as they crawled up into my ear.

"See, my friend, he told me he's been watching you for a while. And he told me," he flicked his eyes toward Main, "he told me he's going to come and collect you today."

Taxi Man didn't look like a weird bat anymore. He was grinning like a cat, the skin pulled away from his teeth, each tooth outlined in a dark, gummy line, his chin elongated into a longer "V." Then he snapped his jaws shut. "I thought you should know."

I jerked the cart. It gave. I tore down the street, my heartbeat was everything, everywhere—in the pavement, in the trees—and it pounded its panic back to me.

But Taxi Man wasn't done. He called after me:

"He'll be driving a white car. Just so you'll know him when you see him."

I turned the corner onto the ridge that ran along the ravine. No way was I looking back.

#4
weird things

It was another weird thing to happen to me in my recent catalogue of weird things to happen to me. Alright, maybe this morning's was the freakiest. After I left Taxi Man and turned onto the ridge, every hair on my body was scorched by panic. But it's not like there haven't been other creeps who have sniffed around where they shouldn't have.

In fact, one of those creeps showed up last Saturday when Alicia and I were doing the Thing That Would Get Her Grounded and, before I go into the details, I have to say it's not like we did something so extreme that Alicia would deserve a month of lost freedoms. For that, you'd think that Mr. Solomon found us doped up in some downtown alley with some drug dealer and a pack of condoms.

Instead, we'd hopped on the Eglinton West bus on a bright Saturday morning hoping for a chance to run into a certain boy at a certain non-competitive indoor track meet. Of course it was about a boy—it was

Alicia after all. I was there to watch the races and okay, maybe to catch a glimpse of R.S. himself. He and Alicia's boy du jour "Blue" (so-named for his blue uniform) were both supposed to be in attendance. But in Alicia's house, you pay if you break Daddy's rules, which included not taking public transit through parts of the city where there have been school shootings or not getting on a bus or subway car where there was some guy who looked like he maybe, sort of, could've been a gang member (just wearing saggy pants and a ball cap counted), which really meant don't take the TTC ever without Mommy or Daddy.

So Alicia and I were on the bus on the hunt for Blue and R.S. Not that I would let it be known that I was on the hunt for anyone. I'm good at not showing what I'm really thinking. It's safer that way.

"We really have to stop using colours as code names," I said to Alicia as we dropped our coins in the box on the nearly empty Eglinton bus. "Why not use a song or a band name as a code?" To me, boys are more like songs than they are colours—any boy worth knowing anyway.

Alicia sighed and said something about me never listening to her. Apparently Blue was his real name (who'd've guessed?): Blue Rodriguez, a junior hurdler from a high school in the east end. His mum came from the same town in Guyana as Alicia's father, but the big selling feature for Alicia were the one-piece spandex suits he wore that emphasized the lines of his thighs with such a dark blue it went into indigo (and once again gave me the opportunity to curse our school colours: pee yellow and poo brown). Who cares? I thought. Another one of Alicia's non-stop crushes.

Anyway, on that day, the day of Alicia's and my great voyage to North York, I would have had to apologize to Mr. Solomon because there happened to be a real threat on the bus.

No one noticed the guy except me. He wasn't obvious—not like one of those people who start burping swear words or lunge at the bus driver—but I knew there was something just a little off about him, like fresh milk as it curdles under your nose.

First, he was the only guy who looked like he was taking the bus for fun. Only the car-deprived take the bus on a Saturday: the old, the young, the single mothers with ten kids, you name it, especially during a snotty Toronto spring.

The guy was across the aisle and two seats back, but I watched his unwanted attention crawl from his blank eyes down his thin lips, slide down his fresh leather jacket into the intentional fade of his jeans, bumping up over the lip of his running shoes, his snappy gym bag sporting a "You Want It, You Get It" sports logo on it, then up and down over the dirty rubber rivulets on the floor until it inched up the aluminium legs of the triple seat that Alicia and I were sitting in.

Alicia was chatting breathlessly about the meet, and would we make it on time because Blue was competing at eleven, and didn't we have to transfer at some point? And how would the bus driver know when we wanted to get off the bus? I answered each question with a quiet voice so Creepy Gym Bag Guy couldn't hear us. Except Alicia started yelling out our destination—York University in the north end of the city—and going on and on like "wasn't our transfer the next stop?" I saw that C.G.B.G. caught the info in his robot eyes, which flicked from us to the greasy patch on the window and back again.

He's probably got a girlfriend who has no idea. Fear and anger were a grass fire in my belly.

Cool it, girl. You're still on the bus. You're still safe.

But for once I wasn't afraid, I was city-born and bred. I knew creeps. Or at least I thought I did. No sweat. I mean, Alicia's kind of oblivious to danger, her face constantly upturned to the sunshine, that kind of thing, so it's up to me to play superhero. And I liked that feeling. Come to think of it, maybe that's why I liked Alicia so much. She made me feel powerful.

We had long ago left the green fields and Lego apartments of Etobicoke. Now we were surrounded by dirty strip malls back-ended by gargantuan apartment complexes. At Jane, a classroom of brassy girls from Little Jamaica got on the bus, their perfumed hair scenting the air. They ignored the bus driver's robotic plea to "move back, move back." By Keele, they had all gone away.

At the gigantic No Frills store that looked like it had been dropped from space into a sea of cracked asphalt, a group of West Indian mothers climbed aboard, juggling children and bags of groceries. A bagful of cantaloupes went bowling to the back of the bus where the baby gangbangers had gathered in a loud posse, but Creepy Gym Bag Guy didn't react; he was too engrossed by his Lolita, Alicia. With three stops to the station, two Hasidic boys with their curls came aboard and took the two-seater behind C.G.B.G, who by then was taking an odd glance at Alicia out of the corner of his eye. The stop after, a white girl who looked no more than nine years old clambered onto the bus, sneaking in from a back door. Her backpack looked like it weighed more than she did. Still she soldiered to the seat across the aisle from C.G.B.G., her black pigtails hanging down her sides. Her muddy shoes didn't even touch the floor. Again, C.G.B.G. didn't pay her or her bone-white skin or her flashing white leggings any mind. Even with a bus growing as we headed to midtown, his eyes were latched only on Alicia as she then stood, anticipating our stop. He pumped his bag in a firm grip, ready to leave, too.

I tapped Alicia's shoulder.

"Naw, we're staying on until Yonge."

At this hour, Yonge would be packed with traffic and people. It would be easy to lose C.G.B.G.

Alicia was immediately annoyed.

"You told me it was Eglinton West."

C.G.B.G. was smoothing the stitched logo of his gym bag, but I knew he was listening.

"Trust me, the Yonge line is quicker," I said.

Alicia sat down, but her face was screwed up with confusion.

"I don't get it."

I put my mouth to her ear. "Creepy guy at two o'clock."

Oh, the eye-rolling.

"Whatever," shrugs Alicia. "You see them everywhere."

Even though I resented this, I was too good a friend to point out that Alicia saw babes everywhere, and too superfine a pal to divulge that I really only became an expert in identifying creepy guys after the whole Matt incident that she was, in part, responsible for.

The bus turned into the metal and glass tent of the Eglinton West station—our stop.

"This is the plan," I mumbled. "Either we stay on until Yonge or we wait until the very last minute and we get off this bus."

"Why do you always have to get freaky all the time?" shot back Alicia. "We're supposed to be having fun today. I'm the one who should be paranoid. Two guesses what happens to me if my dad finds out where I am?"

I felt my ears redden. People got up and shot us

funny looks as they ambled to the exits. The bus was pulling into its slot and still C.G.B.G. was looking at us and a Transit Poetry ad at the same time.

Alicia rolled a caramel eye into her impossibly long lashes.

"Why did I invite you?" she murmured.

I broke my gaze with C.G.B.G. "Come on," I elbowed her. "Aren't I your best friend forever?"

Alicia flicked her eyes to the window, nodding and laughing.

I gave C.G.B.G. a bugged-out look—not imaginative, I know, but slightly effective. He stared down at his sneaker tops. The bus came to a stop. The doors opened and stayed so after most of the bus disembarked, including the driver, a walking stick of a man with spray-painted black hair who hopped over to a vending machine on the platform. The gangbanger wannabes cried out: "Ah, come on man!" then got on their cellphones to complain to friends. The Hasidic boys leaned in for a whisper. Pigtails Girl swung her legs so ferociously that chunks of dried mud started to fly off her shoes.

"Okay, this is the plan," I whispered to Alicia. "Let's wait until the very last minute and then we'll get off, okay?"

"No, I'm staying on until Yonge," sassed Alicia, looking at the advertisements, out the bus window, at anything except the people in the bus. "Isn't that where we're going?"

"Whatever, it's your day," I muttered and settled back in my seat. C.G.B.G. also sat back in his seat, setting his gym bag back on the floor, which didn't make me feel any better.

I've got my eye on you, buddy, I told him silently.

Even Pigtails Girl knew what was going on. She cracked her gum, and looked from C.G.B.G. to Alicia and me, waiting for the showdown.

"It's your day too, except you want to ruin it," whispered Alicia.

"Not true," I said, arms crossed.

The bus driver jumped back on the bus with two bottles of water in each fist. He released the lock on the accordion doors, pulling them closed. Finally, Alicia leaned over and looked down the barrel of the bus. I heard a gasp. "*Ohmigod.*" Before I knew it, a hand was in mine and bending my arm back, nearly out of the socket. I barely had enough time to grab my backpack as the hand pulled me out of the bus, a set of feet jumped on the steps to launch open the doors and the next thing I knew, Alicia and I were safe on the platform, watching the bus pull away with a surprised Creepy Gym Bag Guy confused and annoyed through the grimy window. I couldn't help but wave goodbye to him with a grin. I turned to a clearly elated Alicia, whose left cheek spasmed with nervousness right near her fuzzy mole.

"Geez, you could've warned me," I teased her. Alicia was gnawing the inside of her cheek. She stared after the bus until it wound around the station and caterpillared down Eglinton.

When she did speak her voice was thick and odd: "We get on the subway here, right?"

"Yeah."

"Let's get out of here." Following behind Alicia, I saw her spine twitch and shiver.

I didn't pry her for more information and she wasn't spilling, and, being Alicia, the greyness of her skin, like her mood, returned to its usual warmth on the lurching ride north, and she was back to talking breathlessly about Blue. And then, when we got there, everything became about R.S. I forgot about the creep on the bus, she forgot her mood, and we both admired R.S., aka Red Shortz, who still had his nickname because his real one was kind of average. She did her admiring out loud, and to her best friend, me. As for me, watching R.S., I was suddenly and painfully aware that I was a coward who was secretly lusting after one of her best friend's crushes.

So I've beaten creeps before, in this case, Creepy Gym Bag Guy. In the end it was a bitter victory, because my mum had called Alicia's looking for me and the jig was up with her father. Mr. Solomon went crazy and *guess what*? Alicia blamed me. You could say that was the beginning of the end of our friendship.

After what could have been a great day had finished exploding all over us and I stood guilty and accused, yet another weird thing happened. As mad as she was, later that night Alicia sent me a text message on a scammed cellphone in her locked bedroom. It went like this:

"i thot i saw someone on bus."

"who?" I wrote back. My eyes had been fixated on that creepy guy. I didn't remember seeing anyone I knew on the bus.

"grl"

"wot grl?"

Forever passed before she responded. "u know . . . v."

Otherwise known as Girl #1.

#5
alone on the street

But that was last week and this morning all I could think about after I left Taxi Man was biking like a fiend. It was only after I turned another corner and biked up onto the ridge, when my cart flipped over and skidded on the road that I stopped.

Breathe, girl.

In races, I do that, too. I get so nervous, I forget to breathe and I run off the track lanes in a panic. Generally speaking, it only happens at the really big meets. I can handle the pressure at the small Etobicoke ones. Still, there I was, hunched over Ripley, hyperventilating. What was I going to do now?

I turned to look over my shoulder for Taxi Man but he was long gone. Now that I'd stopped, I couldn't move, and my nerves felt like they'd been cut off from my skin. I couldn't feel the March wind cut under my hat, couldn't feel the pavement underneath my feet or the cool rubber of my handlebars. I was dimly aware that a part of my brain was shouting these sensations

back to me, but I'd put them on mute while I handed
the mic to a phantom voice playing newscaster:

*"Witnesses reported a taxicab idling on Main near
where fourteen-year-old papergirl Syd Johansen was
abducted. Witnesses later reported seeing the cab at a
doughnut shop under the 401 underpass in south Rexdale where a wiry man with bat-like eyebrows who'd
clearly had too many coffees muttered about his
friend, The Collector."*

He's going to collect me.

In a really screwed up way, you'd think I'd have
been happy. It occurred to my feverish brain that I
finally had a major way out of the wedding that no
one could deny: A creepy collector man's gonna collect
me, Mum! His vampire friend drove up in a taxi and
told me so!

*Stop being stupid! This is serious. I should tell
somebody, right?*

A butterfly of fear was let loose in my belly as I
stood frozen on the ridge, my cart in my hand, con-
templating biking forward or beelining it home. But
after I played back Taxi Man's words a zillion times
over in my head, it sounded like such a lie. I mean,
what sane adult would believe that story? I could
imagine answering the cop after I had dialed 911—the
cop looking a bit like super-serious Officer Murdoch
who came to our school to warn us about "The Dangers of Drugs" after three kids were caught selling
dope at the last school dance. Officer Murdoch was a

guy who needled you with his eyes until you shrunk to mouse-hole size. The interrogation would go like this:

Q: Did you get a licence plate number?

A: Uh . . . it was kind of foggy. I didn't see much.

Q: You mentioned it was a cab. What company was it?

A: The kind that has blue *cars*?

Q: Do you have a description of this man?

Would I tell him about the bat-wing eyebrows and vampire accent? Then I would feel so stupid that all I could do would be to stare at the tops of my sneakers until I burned a hole in the toe.

The cop would sigh heavily. Teenagers! He'd raise an eyebrow in a supreme arch, which then would turn into one of my mother's perfectly painted brows over that perfected needling black-eye gaze she has.

"You'd do anything to get out of this wedding, wouldn't you?" she'd accuse me after we got home from the police station.

Yes! I'd fake bulimic spells, shred my junior bridesmaid dress, and run off to a faraway place where it actually *is* spring and there's a green valley I could run and bike in always. And there are no such things as Peterson Weddings or absent fathers and their haggish, mysterious second wives, or neurotic single mothers.

Except that I wouldn't do any of that at all. Essentially I'm a good girl who ends up doing the right thing—*always*. (Note: This is the real reason I've never had a boyfriend.)

But I've tried to do that before. I tried to be a good kid and "tell someone!" And I'm not even going to rant about how unhelpful Mum was when a certain "beautiful" (according to Alicia) boy got hold of my cellphone number at the last dance and began leaving threatening messages that drilled into my gut—another upsetting incident. But so much for Mum. She actually asked if maybe I was imagining things.

I could bike home, cart of papers in hand, and phone Gord-O. Except his mouth would be so full of doughnut holes on his end of the line I wouldn't be able to understand if he was being sympathetic and telling me he'd do the route instead, and go to the cops with me. Maybe he'd just get a case of the burps and tell me I was *imagining* things.

Sorry. That's just being mean. See? Good girl! I apologize when I'm mean. Thing is, even if Gord-O could help me, he tends to turn off his cellphone after he's dropped off his bundles, and mine is one of his last before he heads off to Canadian Tire for his other job in the customer service department. Mum and I had to return a defective coffeemaker to Gord-O last fall. She made a scene when he wouldn't take it back because she didn't have the receipt. It was the beginning of Mum's new high-strung phase—*so* embarrassing.

Back on earth, dawn had now officially broken, and precious minutes were ticking by. I was still frozen, undecided, when I felt a whisper in the wind that sent a chill down my neck.

Behind me the street narrowed then bulged like an overstretched balloon. I was a speck on a road lined with sleeping houses that were creeping away from me, their eyes firmly shut.

This is what it feels like, to be alone on the road or on a bike path, and know that there is absolutely no one who will help you. It's just you and the guy who says he's coming to get you or the one who is harassing you so bad your intestines drop to the ground in fear—game over. All the people who might help you are far, far away. Yeah, I can tell you, it's the loneliest place in the world.

Front page flashes of Girl #1 and Girl #2 appeared before me. Maybe this was how they felt? Alone . . .

No. That's too intense! Transylvania Taxi Man is a *liar*! I've dealt with creeps before. Alicia and I foiled Creepy Gym Bag Man, I thought. I'll be fine.

And like I said, even if I told someone, who would believe me?

Exactly! Rely on yourself. Do your job, keep your job, and get home in plenty of time to get dolled up for the rehearsal. No worries. It'll be easy.

Decided, I reached for the cool handle of my cart with new determination. I found its rattle cutting through the morning quiet reassuring. It's just you and me, kiddo, I thought as I patted Ripley.

In my next life, I'll be a bad girl, I swear.

Because now I know that good girls finish last. Or dead.

#6,
the plan

At that time, I still had one up on White Car Man. I knew he was coming.

That is, I couldn't help thinking, if there was a White Car Man at all. Because maybe Taxi Man was a freak who drove around on weekend mornings and threatened girls just to see them squirm. You know, copycat following the case of Girl #2. Could happen. Still, just to be safe . . .

"I need a plan," I told the pavement.

A squirrel jumped from a dead tree branch and scurried across my path, making me swerve.

"Someone's listening," I muttered, heart in my throat.

On a normal day, I delivered papers along Ravine Ridge, the one straight, long road that cut sense through a maze of crescents, piled on top and humping each other like rabbits in a cage. Then I'd follow all those crazy crescents, the last one coming out at a metal fence beside the entrance to the ravine. Sometimes when I ended my route, I'd throw my folded cart over a shoulder and hurtle down the path to the green below, each bump on Ripley's chunky tires reverberating through my bones.

So here's the situation: Pine was the only street that connected Ravine Ridge to Main. It was the only way that White Car Man could creep his way to me. So, I needed to keep an eye on Pine—*just in case*.

"And what if he came?" my panicky voice kicked in. Okay, I'd be ready with my plan: a series of carefully thought-out escape routes.

Escape plan #1: I'd run into the ravine. A car couldn't follow me down the deep slope of the ravine.

But a man could chase me on foot. He could tear out of his car and run after me, his slippery sneakers tearing up the muddy path. He could reach out and grab my windbreaker and I'd fall, fall like I did last summer, crashing to the ground, rocks scraping elbows and knees or my temple—*bang*! One sharp hit there and you're dead, or one dull hit and I'm knocked out, my head thick with sleep and then I'd wake up and I'd be in the cold cellar of my uncle's house (like Girl #1).

I looked back up Pine. The sun had risen and shone now like a bleak bulb over the street. A curl of still-icy wind tickled the fringe on my forehead. It wasn't too late to bike home, forget my papers, call it off.

No way! I'm not going to end up working at Mum's boutique! If I'm on Ripley, I'll try Escape plan

#2: Spirit away on my bike. Speed down the warped pathways like I'm in the Tour de France. White Car Man doesn't stand a chance! If he's coming. Right?

That's it. I had no other escape plans. So much for my series. My only option was forward.

As I pedalled along Ravine Ridge, my panic lessened. The papers strained my arm but as long as I could will my skinny bicep to hold the cart at a forty-five-degree angle, the cart wouldn't tip over. As long as I kept my arm out at a ninety-degree crook, the inner wheel of the cart wouldn't tear pieces of metal from Ripley's bike pedal or my gearshift.

As long as White Car Man didn't come, I would be fine.

#7
girl #1

Of course, I'm not fine. I'm here.

The wind that's crawling up my back has lost its knife edge but I'm still not stupid enough to move an inch. The bush that I'm hiding behind, with its mass of gnarled, leafless branches, is the best camouflage I have—within running distance anyway.

Again, if I had been smart enough to slip my cell in my windbreaker pocket this morning, I could've at least called someone from my not-so-hidden hiding place. Not Mum, who didn't believe me before either, but maybe Alicia. Not that Alicia would be able to leave the house to rescue me. And not that she'd want to, given the grounding incident last week that she still blames me for, and *especially* if she found out about last night.

Behind my closed lids, I picture the two thick arms of the massive birch tree anchored in her backyard. It's a tree that we'd race to climb, each of us taking a branch, until the white bark peeled off in our clawing fists. We'd decided the tree's bent limbs were great for laying on, so we named it the "Cradle Tree." If my eyes were open, the Cradle Tree would be just out of my actual sightline—tucked away three houses in from the bungalow on the corner that's hidden under a trio of massive evergreens—but close enough to imagine shimmying up into its higher branches.

Looking down from that spot, I'd see Alicia miserable in her sprawling room in the basement, hunched over her neon purple and green paisley comforter, her walls plastered with posters of American basketball stars. ("They don't sell posters of sprinters," she always complains.) She'd feel the vibration of my phone ringing hers. She'd listen hard for her dad's booming laugh or her mum's nasal clucks anywhere in the vicinity of her room before pulling out her banned cellphone, which she would turn on to receive my message.

"Save me!" I would say "Not far. In a bush. WHITE CAR! Call 911."

Or maybe I would call 911 directly. Duh. Except White Car Man would hear me. Could I text 911?

Whatever! Like I said, I didn't bring my cell, so no 911. Plus I'm a bigger traitor than Alicia knows.

Still, I try in vain to send her a psychic plea, up over the Cradle Tree, up over *his* head. C'mon! Doesn't she remember she thought she saw Girl #1 on the bus last weekend? And I saw Girl #2 in the ravine! We're linked, she and I.

Hear me! Feel me!
Nothing.

I think back to that day on the bus, and Alicia's text message afterward. That girl she was talking about, the one on her mind, was Girl #1. Like me, like Mum, Alicia has her secrets, too. Unlike the strangers who lined up for Girl #1's funeral and the ones who wrote cards and stories and poems about her, and all the crying people that they showed on the news, Alicia had actually known Girl #1. And that knowledge ran deep. I'm still freaked out about Girl #1 and I just read about her in the paper like everybody else.

It's not something that I got a lot of details about, trust me. All I knew in the early days after Alicia had transferred to Lucy Maud Montgomery Middle School for grade eight was that the new girl had gone to the same public school as Girl #1 back in Scarborough. The rumours of how well New Girl knew Girl #1 stirred up every clique from the Bare Belly Girls to the Berserker Boys in the Back. You know, for the "wow" factor ("you knew a *dead* person?").

Like usual, I kept my head down and my mouth shut. Under the radar. But that was before I knew the arrival of the New Girl would be the best thing, the first truly great big happy thing to happen to me since, well, since before Dad had left.

This is the way it all went down: I'm twelve, in grade seven, and I find out two weeks after Christmas that Dad, who just divorced my mother, had moved to the States. I mean, he was already gone, but now he was leaving the country! In March, Girl #1 went missing. In April, Ms. Cavanaugh convinced me to try out for the track team after I smoked the grade-seven boys in a "fun run" in the fields under the hydro towers. In May, I won my first ribbons at my first couple of meets (okay—not first place, but second and third aren't bad). In June, Mum had a minor breakdown and The Bride started coming over—way too much. She spent the summer patting my hand and looking sympathetic in this awful, strained way while Mum wore a pyramid of ice cubes for her "migraine." The only good thing was The Bride made me super strawberry milkshakes with real ice cream instead of Mum's ice-water yogurt.

Anyway, September rolls around and just as I'm *loathing* being back in school because I have no real friends again this year, sunny Alicia Solomon arrives. I watched her discreetly. Everywhere she went she was followed by prickly trails of whispers. At first it looked like she was oblivious, but I heard them:

"New girl. New girl . . . kind of pretty. I guess . . . Nah, more like perky—if you like jocks."

Then one Wednesday morning, she talked to me.

"Is anyone sitting here?" Alicia asked, pointing to the seat beside me in the second row of Ms. Cavanaugh's phys. ed. class. There were plenty of empty seats in the front row because the whole class of girls was dreading what would follow—part one of the awful annual sex ed class.

Still, there were others she could have sat beside.
Pretty brainiac Marijo. The strangely mannish Karina.
She could have sat in the back with the snarky Tube
Top Girls (including Melissa). They were responsible
for most of the whispers until they decided they
wanted to induct her into their little club.

Instead, Alicia chose me. Funnily enough, it was
my "uniform" that reeled her in.

"Cool pants," she said approvingly, before intro-
ducing herself.

Word up for baggy, black Adidas! Take *that*, Mum!

I murmured: "I'm Sidonia."

Instead of the usual "Uh, what?" or the extreme
"Omigawd, what a pretty-pretty-girl name!" Alicia's
response made me love her instantly:

"Cool name! So do your friends call you Syd for
short?"

"Syd" was cool. Why hadn't I thought of Syd?
They liked Siddy-Siddy, sometimes Siddy-Siddy-Bang-
Bang, the odd time Doanie-Doanie (which was un-
believably bad) and once I was called something that
rhymes with "Siddy-Siddy," but that was by one of the
Berserker Boys. He punctuated the words by hawking
a loogie into the corner and got sent to the office after
he said it (I don't think they cared he insulted me, it
was that they thought he was showboating with the
spitting).

But no one had thought of Syd, including me. And
it was perfect.

"Yes," I said, and smiled. "That's *exactly* what my best friends call me."

The Bare Belly Girls with their fake and one real navel piercings started up their whispers in the back.

"Oh yeah, I mean, look at those pants. They're, like, to her neck . . . And the shoes! Oh yeah, white no-names: nice. Forget it!"

Then Ms. Cavanaugh entered the class and subjected us to line drawing after line drawing of internal sex organs magnified to extreme extremes on the overhead projector. Each point of her wand was met with giggles or sighs, except by Alicia who raised her hand each time Ms. Cavanaugh asked something.

"Those are vas deferens," Alicia said nonchalantly while we cringed. "They're named after some Dutch explorer, I think. Some guy like Fraser."

I coughed violently into my hand then bit into my palm to stop erupting into laughter while most of the class lost control. Alicia has such balls around adults. Ms. Cavanaugh was left whining over a half-hysterical class.

"Girls, I *have* to teach this."

The whispers started up again.

"Hey, you know she went to that school—the one that that missing girl went to. The one they . . . found . . . No *way*!"

Alicia never heard them. Or at least she acted like it. But her body language screamed "Don't Go There." So I didn't.

When school was over that Wednesday she asked me to come to her house. I jumped at the chance.

That's when I found out all about Alicia and Girl #1.

Alicia's mum, Mrs. Solomon ("Call me Bea, Sidonia"), spilled the beans about Girl #1 while Alicia was upstairs changing, offering me a plate of her burnt multi-grain cookies as she leaked the story. Call-me-Bea's voice had dropped to a hollowed echo as she relayed the details.

"You know, she and Alicia went to the same ballet class when they were just little. I think they were six . . . and then they were in every class together until . . . well . . ." (Alicia did ballet. . . . !?)

When Alicia bounded back down the stairs with a grin, Bea shut up and pasted one on her face, offering her daughter one of the burnt cookies with chewy half-cooked insides I was politely trying to digest. Alicia not-so-politely declined.

"Uh, gross, Mom . . ."

Maybe the fact that Alicia, in her own way, finally admitted to me that she knew Girl #1 was a sign that *he* was coming. Maybe I was being warned, like she was warned, before she grabbed my hand and got us the hell off that bus.

#8
a car on the street

So I'm sure you've guessed. I'm crouched in this bush because I'm hiding out. I may be rambling but you're the unfortunate soul I'm telling my story to, so you'd better get all the details right because I might not be around to correct you.

Halfway through delivering my papers the sun had finally burned off the fog. Its rays cast a dull yellow tinge over the dark bungalow roofs dwarfed by the trees that lined the upper edge of the ravine. I could sense people stirring inside their houses, making that first pot of coffee, but so far no one had greeted me at the door to welcome their Saturday paper. Pretty typical—it wasn't like their regular paper that they pay for. For a lot of them, I might as well have been delivering junk mail, which is accurate, because flyers is exactly what the Saturday *Carrier* is packed with.

Once I decided to get serious and just do it, I'd done most of my route in record time. Another perfect performance from Super-Papergirl, Syd Johansen!

Too bad it wasn't a real paper route, with a real salary. I'd be rich. Too bad Taxi Man's words were still gnawing on my brain the whole time.

He's gonna collect you, he's gonna collect you.

But I was following my safety plan as I went (I'm not an idiot). I'd been doing my route in reverse—*just in case*. Placing my cart behind the odd fat dead bush at the bottom of a driveway, not *hiding* it, exactly, but maybe camouflaging it so you couldn't see it from the road—*just in case*. Bringing my trusted Ripley as close as possible to the doorway of each house, sometimes all the way up the pebbled path to the screen door, or where I couldn't fit past the cars in the drive, laying her down, hidden in front of their grills—*just in case* he came and I was caught at the door of a house while Ripley lay on the sidewalk, vulnerable, out in the open where he could grab her and throw my "getaway car" into his trunk. With each new street, I'd plot out a new escape route—just in case Taxi Man wasn't lying.

Just in case the white car came.

Adrenaline beat a panic in my veins as I turned the corner and started Cedar Crescent. I was starting to agree with that nagging voice inside my head, trying to calm me down by insisting that he wasn't coming, that I was an idiot and a chicken ...

That last thought occurred to me just moments before I saw the car.

It was an unremarkable car. I couldn't tell what colour it was—white, grey, skin tone? Don't ask me what make it was—American? With a fat metal grill and lolling winter tires it made a drunken right turn onto the far end of the crescent.

God, it almost took out a garbage can at the house on the corner! Is a blind person driving? I watched as the car lurched sharply left, attempting to follow the hard curve of the crescent but not having much luck.

With my heart pounding so loud it was rattling the whole street, I enacted General Escape Plan for Cedar Crescent. I had already placed my cart behind a nice fat bush at 23 Cedar—*check*! I had three papers curled under my arm, and with the other hand gripping my bike handles, I scooted up the driveway of 25 Cedar, flew across the circular patio stones, past the front steps, and curled neatly around the side of the house, where I crouched behind a tall Japanese yew, Ripley thrown to the ground beside me (sorry, girl).

I waited and watched, counting each second with the beating of my heart. In my reduced view of the street, I could see nothing for seconds, maybe a minute even; in my head I counted "one-two-one-two-one-two..."

Then the car lurched into view, coming to a halt halfway between numbers 23 and 25. The bike wheel beside me was still rotating from my cruel throw, and I reached over to stop it. From my vantage point the car looked more like tan. Definitely not white, but maybe it was just really dirty? In fact—I had a crazy thought—maybe the car was driven by Dad. Maybe Dad was coming to save me.

The vein that wrapped around my right eye shuddered until my eye ran wet with tears.

Whoa! Where did that come from?

Well, he might be in Toronto for the wedding, and if he was he might be driving a rental (see the peeling rental sticker on the car's bumper?) and Dad gets up almost pre-dawn, which is like two hours before Mum. He used to help me on my route, remember? I mean, he's the reason I actually got the route, since he delivered papers when he was a boy. He was the one who argued with Mum for days that a paper route would be great for me. She hated the idea: dirt, newsprint, perverts in their bathrobes.

In the beginning we did it together. After I knew all the houses by heart and did it lickety-split, he'd tag behind me in the car on weekends, jug of coffee in one hand, steering wheel in the other. He'd wave and let me know he was up and I was okay. This was our time together. Comfortable in the silence of the neighbourhood, the morning birds, the hum of my old bike's tires . . . and then we'd go back home and feast on banana pancakes (with melted chocolate chips!), all before Mum got up and they started fighting and ruining my day.

Before he took off.

The white-blue-tan car slowed to a park. The passenger door opened and I caught a flash of metal, like a length of pipe, maybe. I ducked down quick, like I'd been struck by it. The person holding the pipe rocked back and forth, back and forth in my line of vision. I checked back over my shoulder. In the narrow alley behind me there was a tall pine fence that the houses shared. There was a door, but also an iron padlock on the latch. Crap! I could scramble up the fence, I thought, but I'd have to leave my bike behind. Okay, that was the worse-case scenario.

On the street, a second person had climbed out of the driver's car—wait. Taxi Man never said there were *two* people. And it's an *old man*?! In his sixties, seventies, I couldn't tell. He tottered over to the person exiting the passenger seat. I watched as he grabbed her (I was guessing it was a "her" by her pink scarf) by an elbow, as if steadying her on her feet. She staggered forward; she was wearing weird pink glasses that wrapped around her face.

I could hear her voice, like the caw of a crow, from where I was sitting.

"I swear I saw someone."

She was scanning the street through those pink filters. They were like something out of those weird science fiction movies that came on late on weekends. The ones I watched whenever I was too upset to sleep. Which was a lot. Or when I wasn't at school dances. Which was a lot, too.

"You're seeing things, Mildred. Remember your surgery."

I recognized those glasses. They're for cataracts. Great Uncle Morley had to wear them at the last reunion. But his were black.

This was getting too weird.

Mildred cawed again.

"I know what I saw! I know what I see and what I don't see!" She emphasized each syllable by pounding her cane. "And I told you to turn right before we hit Eglinton. Now look where we are!"

Does no one carry maps in this city?

These people were harmless. I stepped out from the bush to look at them, and to give them a look at me. The lady grabbed her chest, pointing at me with her cane and gasping.

"Oh my!"

The husband, who was likely thinking Mildred was having a fit, tried to stuff her, squawking, back into the car, but Mildred was a brick wall. She wasn't goin' anywhere.

"The girl!" Mildred managed to spit out.

I was halfway down the driveway with my same three papers glued to my arm. I couldn't help it. It's the same allure that draws people to traffic accidents. I had to get a closer look at Pink Flapping Cataract Woman and her husband. And I was so very, very relieved, and feeling, maybe, a little stupid. Here's your bogeyman, Syd. Idiot.

The husband finally looked my way, his mouth a frozen "O."

"I told you I saw someone," hissed Mildred. She

continued to not address me directly, even though I'd arrived at the bottom of the driveway, an easy ten feet away from them. "Ask her, Hal," she prodded. "Go on, ask her."

Then she stared at the bush where I'd hidden my cart.

"Um, hello," Hal began formally. "We're looking for Pine Ridge Drive. Are you familiar with this area?"

"Sure," I said, and when they didn't say anything more, I continued. "Pine Ridge is about four blocks away on your left. Just go back on Main, turn left and go past Rathburn about two blocks and it's there."

"I see," said Hal in his weirdly formal manner. He turned to Mildred, like he was gloating. "Not only it is *past* Eglinton, it's past Rathburn, which is even farther than Eglinton."

"I guess," I said, not wanting to get any more involved in their business.

More gloating. "Did you hear that, honey? It's past Rathburn."

"I heard!" Mildred blasted back. "At least I was right about the girl!"

"Yes dear."

I watched as they got back in their car and drove up the still-sleeping street.

I said it in my head after they'd gone: *They were harmless. They drove a tan car. White Car Man, he isn't coming.*

I started to tremble—my fists shook, my knees shook. Taxi Guy was just like Matt, that "beautiful boy" who'd left messages on my cellphone: a bully who used fear to make his victims do whatever he wanted them to do. Hide in the bushes for fear of the bogeyman or run terrified into stranger's houses, just so they could get a laugh.

How dare you, how *dare* you scare me, driving around in your taxi car! How dare you scare me with tales of the White Car Man. Yeah, and don't think I haven't read the papers! You picked the *wrong girl* to mess with! I may be small, but I'm smart as hell. I know what happened to Girl #2 (last seen walking on the Bloor Street Bridge, high above the ravine she would be found in), but didn't they catch that guy after awhile? Didn't they put away him and his friend, who stalked in twos: one lured, the other grabbed? Aren't both of them rotting behind the stone walls of the Don Jail?

Maybe, Taxi Man, you read the story and decided to have some nasty fun. You get off scaring girls, pervert?! *Well, screw you!*

The three papers I had under my arm had taken a beating while I was flailing around and ranting and raving. That's not professional, Syd. I composed myself and took a minute to smooth out their crumpled fronts with a shaking hand. Calm down.

There's no need to adhere to the plan. I'm going to finish delivering my final papers and that'll be it. There's nothing to be afraid of. Right?

#9
~~beautifully~~ awful matt

Although sometimes the people you know are the ones you need to be afraid of the most.

"Who ya looking for, kid?"

That's what the voice in the dark said. It may have been a guy's voice. All I know is it trailed a line of spooky down my neck. I dug my chin into my chest and forced my back against the steel door that led into the gym. It was the first dance of the year—grade nine, high school, the big time. Alicia had abandoned me for the time being, having to bum something or see about a boy or something like that, cheerfully saying, "Just wait, I'll be back," before disappearing into the darkness toward the parking lot, I thought, but who knows? I only agreed to go to this stupid dance if she and I would be glue and she'd dumped me already. Or maybe she's lost.

Slight panic in my chest—the story Alicia told her Dad is that she was sleeping over at my house, which was true. We just didn't mention a dance. And this time Mum was onboard.

"What's so wrong about going to a dance? You girls are smart. Why, when I was your age . . ."

Mum trailed off down memory lane, I tuned out.

Alicia said afterwards, "God, your Mum is so cool. Trade?"

If she only knew: Mum may look divine, but life with just her and me isn't heaven.

The catcalls came from the blackness between where I stood and the wooden stands behind the fir trees; the voices were disguised by the needles and the night.

"Hey kid . . . you waiting for your girlfriend?"

More throaty laughs came from the shadows. I thought I heard a "shut up, man" from his friend, or maybe that was just wishful thinking. The bass pulsated through the door directly into my spine. I couldn't separate the throbbing of the music from a growing, pulsing panic. I zipped my jacket up to my nose, the metal zipper cold on my tongue.

Where the hell was Alicia?

I shuffled my feet, my sneaker catching a beer cap and scraping it against the asphalt. The sound jolted me. More chuckles from the darkness. I could smell a curl of sweet smoke and hear the wooden stands creak under the weight of the boys sitting on them. Those stands were dull and splintered—maybe one of them would snap and they'd fall through, end up on their asses. I could only hope.

"Was that girl your *lu-ver*? Are you a *les-bian*?"

"Can't girls have short hair and wear sweat pants?" I wanted to scream. Welcome to the twenty-first century! I hunched my shoulders up to my ears and casually tested the door with one hand behind my back—still locked. I thought I heard a smack on flesh (maybe wishful thinking) then a gravelly voice (think he was the one who told his friend to shut it) said, not so ghoulishly:

"Hey, are you waiting for someone?"

I answered. I can't believe it.

"My friend Alicia." I didn't really want to have a conversation with these guys, but the words shook out. "Have you seen *her*? She's my height except she has *cornrows*? She was wearing a purple jacket, really *bright*? She went in there."

I pointed into the abyss to the right of the slightly lighter void where the boys' voices seemed to be coming from. God, I sounded like a dim Tight Jeans Girl—acting stupid to get boys, but also because the guy in front of me sounded pretty dumb. But what could I do? Alicia could be so trusting, so boycrazy, so . . . stupid.

"She's a niner, right?" continued the gravelly pretty-much-friendly guy voice.

"Y-aaaaaa?" *Arg! Halt the bimbo drone, Syd!*

The voice emerged from the shadows, attached to a boy. He could have had a nice face if it wasn't covered in long blond bristles that seemed to sprout from every pore. Still, his features were soft and his eyes were wet marbles, sympathetic, saying *get out of here, kid* without uttering a syllable. What he does say is:

"Think I saw her head to the ravine."

That wasn't right. Going to the ravine was a very un-Alicia thing to do. Alicia liked malls and clean carpeted floors, not dirt and mud and tree branches that threatened to catch and accidentally dirty a designer T-shirt sleeve.

Friendly Furry Blond Boy continued his guilty eye dance. "You know Matt?"

Sure (heart flip flop). Matt. Model pretty, grade eleven, and not too tall. Snow White Boy with just something a little sour about him, I thought. Eye teeth just a tad too pointed, bottom lip always moist, like he had just licked it, too red, like he had just eaten steak and the juice soaked in. He played up the good-boy factor just a little too much with teachers and parents. Alicia and every other girl at school gushed over him.

I dubbed Matt "Black" in our list, the colour of his eyes and his hair, natch, and the colour of his dad's first sports car that he would drive the whole four blocks to school in (the same one he'd trash later that night, only to be forgiven and given another one). It was also for the feeling he gave me when we caught glances—electric black.

I waited for Furry Face Boy to finish, while erasing images of Matt toying with Alicia—maybe, well, *using* her.

"I saw her go down into the ravine with Matt. That's all ... she was ... I don't know ..."

"What!?"

Furry Face Boy wouldn't say anything else. I guess I scared him. He shuffled back to his stands to smoke or pick up whatever he was doing before.

This was great. The first school dance of the year—a dance that I had wanted to avoid like the plague—and I had to rescue Alicia from my own blacker-than-black ravine filled with teenagers, drinking, smoking, maybe exchanging bodily fluids.

Should I go find her? Make sure she's okay? It was my ravine, after all, even if I'd never been there at night. No, no. I couldn't breathe. Something bad was going to happen, I just knew it.

What, like third base? Catching Alicia and Matt in a liplock (or something else)?

Stop being a baby. Make sure your best friend isn't in over her head. I closed my eyes and dove into the blackness.

now
2

#10
in hiding

Black. Black's been my colour lately, and here I am in the blackest place I've ever been. And thanks for sticking with me, waiting patiently while I rehash the recent and not-so recent events of my life as it flashes before my eyes.

I was stupid, stupid, stupid. I know this now like a dead truth in my heart. I knew what Matt, a boy on foot, was capable of, knew his reputation, and that should have made me even more terrified about men in cars.

But before I always got away: Alicia and I got away from Creepy Guy, from Matt. I always got us, me, away. And with four papers left for me deliver with White Car Man still not making an appearance, I thought I was safe. I thought Taxi Man was lying. Bluffing. Getting his kicks. And that I was just getting paranoid.

Turns out I'm not paranoid. Creepy Guy was a joke. Matt is an afterthought.

White Car Man, I think he's playing for keeps.
Shh. Maybe he can hear my thoughts.

The icy wind blows across my exposed lower back as I crouch behind a leafless bush on a corner lot, my careful plan in tatters.

An hour ago, I was so confident he would never be coming. You heard me, you know after Mildred and Hal, I was *convinced*.

But that was before I biked onto Ravine Ridge and suddenly, *there he was*—in a car so brightly white you couldn't mistake it for any other colour, white like the clouds would be in summer. And it was a sedan with four doors, metal trim rimming the windows. It was trying to corner me on Ravine Ridge.

How did I know that? How did I know it wasn't another Mildred-and-Hal false alarm? Because you know that gut feeling you get, like you're punched in the stomach and the air's been knocked out of you? Well, I had that feeling about Creepy Guy. About the ravine that night with Matt. When my parents sat me down to say our family was breaking up and my dad was leaving. I trust that feeling.

When White Car Man drove up and that feeling hit me, all I could do was try frantically to find an exit route, but he was blocking the exit, so I turned back into the maze of crescents, biked like hell, picked a bush—any bush—and threw the cart! My brain was screaming: *Pick a house, any sleeping house, throw my bike under a car, hide behind a hedge—found one on the corner!* I slid into it and here I am. Waiting. Watching. *What is he waiting for?*

A thinning evergreen shields me on one side, an old-growth hedge buttresses me on the other. Green buds are just forming in the grey skeleton of branches. If the hedge wasn't an old growth, you could easily see my crouching form with my windbreaker flapping like cardinal red wings from the street. Still, for the time being I'm hidden, and I have a squirrel's-eye view on both streets.

I have no idea how long I've been crouched here, except to say that my sneakers are cemented into the quicksand mud, my leg muscles are threatening to seize from the trembling, and the sun is now completely above the horizon. It must be close to 8 a.m. and I still have three papers to deliver. Crap! Also, my temple feels wet. I touch it with a tap and see fresh blood running over my skin. I must have hit a thorn bush in my scrambling. Then I absently lick my dirty fingers. I taste bitter newsprint cut with the sweet iron taste of my blood.

I exhale through my mouth, like when I'm running: force slow, deep breaths out my mouth, instead of sharp panting. Ms. Cavanaugh used to chide me for hyperventilating at the big meets, but I can't help it: The butterflies in my stomach always consume me. Now I'm thinking: *slow, deep breaths*. How many minutes have I been crouched here, and where is *he*? Last I saw of him he was inching his way down the maze of crescents, and I know that he's going to have to turn around and drive right by the house that I'm hiding beside to get out.

Just stay where you are, girl. There's no telling when he's going to come back.

I suppose I could stand up and stroll over to the front door of the house where I'm hiding. Knock, knock, and . . .

"Excuse me, White Car Man is coming to steal me away. Would you mind if I used your bathroom?"

But the house has a serious buildup of flyers in its rusty mailbox. And even if it didn't, I'm not tempted to move an inch from my hiding spot. This is the best place for me to be. Just wait until he drives by and I'll be safe. I can go back to my normal life.

Salt winds down my cheek. My legs are aching, wobbly.

I *am* smart and I hate you, White Car Man. I'm going to use that hate, whittle it into a red poker of anger. Use it to poke your eyes out, run past you and get the hell out of here.

Just be quiet. He can't see you. But you can see him.

Well, yes and no. I can't see his face. I think I got some of the licence plate. The three numbers at the end, maybe even one or two letters in the beginning, but they dance in my frantic brain, switch places, stand on their head—*Stop it*! Ok, I have, like, a sense of him: he's white, I think. He looks young, I think. God, if only I could see his face . . .

Never mind. Just wait and watch. Wait for his face to come clear and then memorize it. If you can memorize his face you can identify him. You can tell the police.

And right now I know I will go the police. If I get the chance.

Because right now I'm trapped, I have nowhere else to go. I wipe my nose with the back of my reddened hand and wait, eyes wide open. I wait and wait.

#11
girl #2 and me

A funny thing happens when you have an eternity to wait: Your vision, having focused on one point for so long, starts to blur. Strange things appear out of the corner of your eye. Like right now, I could swear that I just saw a young girl sprint from behind the brown station wagon parked in the driveway of the house to my right to the fat fir tree that's staked at their curb, her jean bell-bottoms kicking up gaping holes, her thin red hair a flag in my line of vision. Ice water runs over my skin when I realize I recognize her. Not so strange after all. It's Girl #2. Now I'm positive I saw her last fall.

I close my eyes to stem the wave of nausea that hits me. My brain kicks into recall and I see her in my ravine, mentally flash forward through the front-page stories documenting her fate. I could describe her story in excruciating detail to you, I could describe both of their stories, Girl #1 and Girl #2—from what they looked like, to where they went to school, to what happened *after*—and you'd immediately remember where you were when you read about them. They are that familiar. But there's part of me that wants to protect them. I know, pretty funny—me trembling in the bushes, muscles seized, I can't even tell if I've peed myself—some protector. But you already know the end to their stories—picked over like carrion—so why do you need to hear it again from me?

The thing is, once I start the news recall in my head, I can't stop the overflow: both of their stories, every detail, flits behind my closed lids. I start to whimper in my spot behind the hedge then stop. I can't risk making a sound. Image after image overwhelms me, a steady diet of facts and faces reduced to crude pixels in school photographs that makes me feel ill.

I open my eyes—nausea has my world spinning. I have to drop my head to focus on anything. My gaze lands on the rubber tips of my sneakers and the new gashes on them. I stare at the ripped rubber until my vision steadies.

Girl #2: Did I tell you I cut off my hair when they found her? I didn't think the two incidents were connected at the time: me going for the shorn look and her, the quirky tomboy whom, in another life I might have been friends with—found, you know, where they found her (like a cocoon in a tree: white bed sheets and mud and twigs and strands of red hairs breaking away).

At the time, I needed a change. It was two weeks after the stupid Matt thing.

"Want some more?" Matt whispered in the halls the whole month after.

At least I think it was him, the whispers materialized when I least expected them: a chuckle in a washroom stall, a hiss coming from girls huddled around a locker. The whispers weren't that frequent—just enough—and each time they burned my ears.

Anyhow, I cut my hair. I was actually a couple of inches away from shaving it all off. I thought my newly shorn scalp looked cool, clean. I teased my fingers across the short, sharp surface, saw the bumps of my scalp previously camouflaged under a mat of hair.

Mum screamed when she walked in—*unannounced*, I might add. She fell to her stocking knees, clutching at fallen snatches of my hair, cherry strands with black roots against the gleaming white tiles, more than a failed dye experiment; in fact, it had been too successful. It drew Matt to me, didn't it? There was so much of it! Mum couldn't contain it all, not on her lap anyway, where she clumsily piled it. Mum, who never allowed a stray hair to settle on any article of clothing or piece of furniture, was frantically gathering all my cut strands into a pile as if she could magically affix the mass to my scalp and I'd be female with a capital "F" once again.

This will make them leave you alone, I remember thinking, looking in the mirror. You look dangerous. They won't mess with you.

And it was true. All the guys, and even the girls,

save for Alicia, cut a wide berth around me. Alicia
rubbed my head and called me a freak but she said it
with typical Alicia brightness and a clear fondness that
said I was her freak. Mum started to cut a berth
around me too. No more snuggles on the couch, com-
miserating over Dad leaving us as we watched *Saturday Night at the Movies* (or as Mum calls it, *Magic
Shadows*). Good, it served her right. Maybe if she was
normal, he wouldn't have left. Anyway, it was a relief
to be left alone. I was getting too much love already
from guidance counsellors asking me if I needed real
counselling from like, professionals.

My hair's grown back now. But Girl #2 still knows
me because she's standing to my left, her hands cupped
as she peers through the twine of dead branches. She's
staring right at me. Well—and this is creepy—kind of
through me. The entire left side of my body gets all
tingly, like microscopic ants are running along my
flesh. If I wasn't feeling cagey before, now I have the
urge to spring up and shoo her away. For my safety,
not hers—obviously.

*Go away! He'll see you and then he'll know I'm
hiding here!*

It's like she can read my thoughts. She turns and
resumes her run along the sidewalk, heading to No
Man's Land, the entrance to the ravine. If she veers to
her left, she'll fall off the sidewalk and tumble right
into the trees. Wait a second, if she disappeared again,
where would that leave me? I want to cry out.

Wait! Tell me what to do! No one else is here to save me!

But she's already gone. Still, Girl #2 has shown herself to me not once but twice. There's no way my brain is making this up. But why would the ghost or spirit or whatever of Girl #2 materialize around me again?

Of course they found Girl #2's body in her ravine, but she was last spotted on the bridge that spans the chasm of the Don—its canopy of white toothpicks is supposed to discourage people from jumping to their deaths. They weren't much of a deterrent for perverts looking to snuff out little girls though.

According to the newspaper reports the police think Girl #2 walked past the toothpicks, maybe listening to some tunes on headphones. She didn't even make it to the first street past the bridge. The men in the car must have caught her before the on-ramp to the parkway below and they dragged Ra—.

Oh—you almost got me there. I almost told you her name and once I tell you her name, all the details of her life will rush into the front of your brain. So I'm not going to tell you her name. I'm going to respect her privacy. The way I would want mine respected if it happened to me.

Is it happening to me?!

One of the other reports was about the suspects. Seems police thought she might have known them. Like Girl #1 and her uncle. Or at least that's the theory, you know, because they like to find similarities. Things that make sense when things happen that don't.

Maybe they *do* always know them. Okay, well not always, but sometimes—a lot.

I hunch my legs in a deeper squat, my knees creaking in complaint. Maybe I know who this White Car Man is. Thing is, I know the face of every person who lives on my street and the street behind mine. I remember the face of every boy I've thought was cute or clever or who shouted out "Hey Baby" or "Lesbo." And I have never seen Taxi Man, who's obviously working with White Car Man, before. I am positive of this. I am not capable of forgetting a face. As for White Car Man . . . if only I could get a look at his face . . .

Hey, wait a minute, what's the colour of Matt's dad's new sports car? It could be white, or maybe he was using his friend Cam's car?

And I know he lives just around the bend from Alicia's house, except his has been gutted and rebuilt so it's twice the size. I've seen him chat up the neighbourhood mums, making them forget their thickened waists, the orange neon of their tanning-salon skin, but I read the underside to his words (even tasted the underside of his breath) and right now he may very well be in the White Car at the end of the dead end waiting for me, having one last laugh at little Syd.

She may have sliced off that pretty girl hair, she

may pretend to be tough, but I can still get to her.

Is Matt's new car white?

It could very well be. I play back all of Alicia's deluded murmurings about Matt, although they pretty much dried up after the night in the Hornet's Nest. Course, that was probably because I wouldn't listen to her talk about how great he is. Even if Alicia was still harbouring her secret devotion to Matt, I would be the last one she'd admit it to.

Wait a minute, this doesn't make sense. No way would Matt be working with a taxi driver. I bet he's never taken a cab in his entire privileged life!

The wind rustles my windbreaker. It's very quiet. Maybe White Car Man is gone already. He didn't win, he didn't get me! Should I wait until my legs seize for good and I can't move? No.

I fill my lungs with courage, command my legs to unfurl, and stand up from behind the bush. I look out onto this stretch of grey suburban road to see if I'm safe.

#12
white car man

Eiiiiiiiiii! He is there! He is there! He is there! He is right in front of me and *he is there! He is there! He is there* looking through the thinning fir branches, *he's zeroed in on* my eyes! He seems to tower over me, but he isn't that tall really because I haven't unfolded my legs all the way. The bastard snuck up on me and now I can't see his White Car anywhere.

And he has locked onto me. *He is there! He is there!* He is there standing in front of me. And his face ... do I know him?!

Girl ... ,

... there isn't anything to describe, nothing I could describe even if I did make it out and was able to tell a policeman who believed me.

Girl!

It's like he doesn't have a face; at least not any facial features.

There's his hair, dirty blond, cut like a catalogue

model, parted to the side. There's the point where his shirt touches his Adam's apple—a white T-shirt under a clean blue plaid lumberjack shirt—but everything in between, from the line of his chin to his forehead, from his ear to ear, is blank. It's as if his face is carved from wood but the carver stopped his digging and didn't cut a mouth or nostrils, didn't set in the wet eyes. I'm so panicked I can't make it out. Everything's a blur.

Syd!

I'm mesmerized by White Car Man's lack of a face. There is a slope for a nose, there are ridges for eyebrows and cheeks, there are holes chipped out for eyes, but there is nothing distinguishable: only bland, beige smoothness. Still, it coughs uncomfortably, it emits concern when it says, "Can you help me?"

You gotta move! *Move* now!

He takes one step. And that's all it takes. And I know I only have one place that I can go.

"I know about you!" I blurt out. Then I turn around and bolt, down along the hedge to the minuscule opening where the hedge and the owner's back fence don't quite meet up. Dead branches rip red lines across my face, the ground a blur of mud and mulched leaves until I hit sidewalk—now a grey-black-white blur under my feet.

This is the direction Girl #2 ran, she was heading for the ravine—was she helping me, showing me how to escape? Just like how Alicia acted on the bus after she thought she saw Girl #1, a time that now seems years and years ago? Asphalt bleeds into concrete curbs and sidewalks—then I'm in No Man's Land, a bright bull's eye on a grey canvas, but I can make it— I'm so fast!

You can outrun him! No one *can catch you!*

Out of the corner of my eye I see White Car Man, unsure, breaking into a run, then skidding to a full stop, running fingers through his hair—what to do?

He's giving you time! Use it!

I keep my direction full-on forward, but a quick look back confirms that White Car Man is committed to following me. My running shoes dig into fertile earth—brown and barely green—my rubber soles sliding through newly thawed dirt down a bumpy path. The forest opens its doors to me first—they're *my* woods, after all. I run down its treed hills to the ravine, to its bundles of thorny thickets and its maze of dirt pathways beyond the stream. *my* ravine.

Come and get me.

#13
r.s.

My recent past is flashing in front of my eyes again, and I grab onto it, because even though I know Alicia won't want to be my friend again once she finds this out, it's a good memory, and if this is it, this is the thought I want to go out on—last night's yellowed popcorn and a guy named R.S.

Now that I've stopped running, and, in fact, I'm within attacking distance of Faceless Man (formerly White Car Man, and more on where I am later), I might as well spill.

See, I did go to that dance last night. The one that I told Alicia I wouldn't go to, not even to suck up because she thinks she got grounded because of me the week before. I said she could hang out to make her father think she *was* studying, but there would be no dance. That's when she told me to screw myself and stomped home fuming and hating me even more.

As a friend, that was strike number two.

I really was not going to go. Then the phone rang

and I knew in that sixth-sense kind of way that if it wasn't Dad ("416," "647," or *long distance*?), it was about Dad. I didn't need to tiptoe to the bottom of the stairs and listen to the elevated shrieking voice Mum used whenever she talked to or about him to know. Her shriek had infected me.

I made a quick stop at our "telephone message centre" and scribbled a note to Mum:

"Gone to Dance. At school. Back at 11."

Okay, maybe a part of me, just an *inch*, thought what Alicia and all the other swoony girls were saying was true: that someone with the initials R.S. would be at the dance. And suddenly I didn't care how she felt about him. I cared about how he made me feel—like wanting to go to a dance again.

Truly cool kids and drugged-out losers show up late to dances. The cool kids have friends, parties, all that, to get primed. The losers get hammered in a parking lot then show up late, only to (maybe) puke in a garbage can.

I didn't belong to either group but there I was, weaving around the groups of the giggly, the drooling, the delirious, and the angry, set out like bombs in the parking lot, just to get to the main entrance.

For once I thought I looked good, and I cared about looking that way—new black Adidas jacket, black jeans, and a white T-shirt. When in doubt, go with black and white, right? It's classic.

Most of the bad and cool and drunk and whatever groups gathered around the cars so I zipped up my jacket for cover and hunched along the brick wall, head down, mentally melding myself into the dark shadows, past the dark open jaws of the auto-shop bays, until I reached the entrance—home free. I couldn't quite believe my luck.

"Hey, Cherry."

I got rid of the red, jerk! I didn't stick around to see who the voice belonged to, or where it was coming from. It was close enough to be dangerous.

Instead, I took off like I was running a 200-metre race, not slowing down until my sneakers hit the brown splattered tiles of the lobby.

"Is she your *luv-er?*" said the voice in the same menacing intimate tone.

Wait a sec—I'm sheltered under Parkside's brick awning. There's nowhere for Sinister Voice to hide. My mind was playing recall with my memories. Seeing ghosts, hearing ghost voices; I was losing my mind.

Relief washed over my skin and the sweat at my temples started to cool. Deep breath, I thought, flicking my eyes left and right, watching the kids milling under the glazed fluorescent bulbs, giggling in groups, crouched in the corners, conspiring.

What the hell was I doing there anyway? I didn't belong.

Still, I kept going, marching past a dull-eyed Mr.

Kingsely, the evening's chaperone, and a sharp-eyed cop on the lookout for liquor and stumbling kids, until I plowed through the double doors marked "Exit" at the other end of the hallway. The lock closed behind me with a satisfying click—there was no way back in, not that I was tempted.

This was a mistake.

I took a gulp of oxygen, let the tears form silently and roll down my cheek.

That was close.

There was a residue of bile in my mouth. Why did I think it was possible to go by myself to a dance? Without Alicia to pretend that she was the victim who needed me, and not the other way around, I crumbled. I scrunched my fists so deep into my pockets that the lining threatened to rip.

Then I was off and running again, alongside the stone wall that directs students into two lanes. When I hit the end I reached for the metal rail to hop down the few steps. That's when it hit me. Actually, that's when I hit *it*, stumbling over a dark lump that jettisoned me down onto the sidewalk.

Great.

The lump uttered an unimaginative "*Ow!*"

I had managed to land on my left foot My ankle creaked and complained, but I managed to stand and mutter "Sorry" into my zipped-up neck. I was just about to take off again when a flash of light, gold-coloured, caught my eye. I got goose bumps.

No . . . way!

R.S. stood up, giving me a full view of him, long fingers clutching the back of his neck, blond brush-cut catching the glare of the streetlight. He looked impossibly tall, although that could have been because he was still standing on the bottom step and my rubber sneakers were firmly planted on the sidewalk below.

"S-sorry," I said again, stuttering with surprise. Sorry I wrecked your neck. Sorry I'm an idiot and a chicken. Sorry flashbacks of Matt the Freak unnerved me. I stood there stupidly while R.S. tested out his neck. I supposed if I broke it he wouldn't be able to move it, right? I took the movement as a good sign and offered a meek:

"Uh . . . are you okay?"

He managed a squint and a grimace that I took as a signal of health. His facial muscles were working anyway.

"Do I know you?" he asked.

Yes! I'm the best friend-make-that-likely-to-be-former-best-friend of the girl who would be soiling herself if she were in my place right now. Nice to meet you!

"Um, I don't think so," I managed.

He shrugged, like "oh well," as I continued to stand there stupidly, not quite with it. I watched, dumbly, as he ran a quick tongue across his lips.

"I'm waiting for a ride," he said finally, as a point of explanation.

Of course, I thought, but didn't say anything. I didn't want to move. I suppose I was waiting until the discomfort bubble swelled and broke, enveloping both of us in its translucent black stain so I wouldn't have to look him in the face anymore.

R.S. coughed to clear his throat then plunged his hands into his pockets. He offered me a glimmer of an awkward smile as he stepped down, past me, casually looking up the street. For his ride, no doubt. I had to do *something*. If I continued to stand and just stare at him, I wouldn't be able to face him at any future track meet, at any event, ever again.

Say you do track. Say you do track. Say you do track.

"I run track," I blurted out, finally. "I race, I compete, that sort of stuff."

I watched as he halted his exit strategy. He sized me up with a squint.

"Oh, yeah? Me too."

I was dreading another awkward bubble of silence but that was the best I could do! I truly couldn't think of anything else that would sound natural and conversational and not betray the fact that Alicia and I had memorized all his track appearances, his results, his times, his running outfits, the part of his hair. Not betray that—here goes—I *worship* him.

Then, right then, fate intervened. He turned right around and generously rewarded my stupidity with a brilliant, lopsided grin.

"Yeah, yeah! *You're* the girl who broke that record at Etobicokes last fall, right? You lost your shoes."

I reddened then swelled with pride. It was a cross-country race. Super muddy. I lost both shoes in the creek, and ploughed on in brown slimy socks. "Yeah, yeah," I said. My voice steadied. "That was me."

"What's your name again? It's something really different, something long, right?"

God, don't make me utter my opulent, excessive name! I thought. I cursed my mother.

"I know what it is—Ophelia! Right?"

For one horrified moment I thought I was going to laugh so forcefully in his face that I'd spit all over his fine features. Yup, that was me: Ophelia, Hamlet's would-be girlfriend, a love-sick twit who threw herself into the river after Hamlet went cuckoo. Then she drowned herself with flowers entwined in her long flowing locks. She was only the exact opposite of me, with my black hair growing out, my lack of feminine fussiness, my practicality. But wow, my mother would have been impressed.

I bit my lower lip until I tasted blood, but it was better than laughing out loud. R.S. didn't know what to make of my strangled silence.

"What?" he asked, exasperated. "C'mon, help me out here."

"It's Syd," I croaked.

"Just Syd?" Those magnificent eyebrows furrowed in confusion as I mutely cursed my mother some more.

"Yup."

"Okay, whatever. Syd. I'm Ian."

"Ian," I repeated dumbly, but the uttering of it gave me an unmistakeable, illicit thrill.

Ian. Such a nice *normal* nothing name. This is why we had to rechristen him. Careful though, I thought, it looked like my moment of bliss was about to run out. He was back to looking over his shoulder, not obviously, but clearly on the lookout for his ride. As in: get away from this girl!

I cleared my throat. "So you went to the nationals, right?"

I'd caught his interest again. He grinned. "Yeah, I made it for hurdles. Got a bronze." He shrugged, embarrassed. "It wasn't ideal. I completely botched my start."

I would die to have a bronze from the nationals. But I nodded and clucked like it was my tragedy, too.

"So, what about you?" He continued. "Did you go on to the provincials?"

The Ontario finals. I cringed at the memory: There was me, all goose bumps at the starting line, temperature hovering near zero, no gloves, no tights, working myself into an emotional state pre-race.

I tersely shook my head.

"Ah," he said, not pressing me. Then, after a pause: "Yeah, I've had those races, too."

Liar! Golden boys like you never fumble! *You* never have. I could recite your list of city and provincial records like my own vital stats, I thought.

I said nothing out loud, naturally then there we were again: having run out of words. But this time, at least it seemed to me, the silence was more pleasant—a soothing green veil.

Then it happened. Up ahead, a car turns onto the side street from Main, two headlights shining in the short distance. He craned his neck and peered at the car approaching. From here it looked grey-white, like the bleached shell of an insect.

"That's probably my ride," he said.

"Oh." I said. More silence. Then, just when I thought the silence was all the awkwardness I could bear, I blurted out: "Is it your girlfriend?"

I immediately regretted the words.

Ian (I feel a jolt even thinking of this name) cocked his left eyebrow. His eyes narrowed as they assessed me, like suddenly I'm under the orange heat lamps at an all-night buffet. I knew exactly what he was thinking—under that vinyl track top, I was suddenly female, just female enough for him to pause and contemplate. Was I pretty enough for him? Old enough for him? Young enough? Was I too cool, too tomboy, or just the way he liked them? I shuffled from foot to foot, not meeting his eye. *Totally* humiliated.

He was fine, answering (after what seemed like eons) with a simple: "Nah, just a buddy."

And then he was walking kind-of, sort-of toward me, probably because I was standing between him and

the curb, where his (male) buddy would soon drive up.
I mean, it wasn't like he was trying to walk into me on
purpose, but as the car pulled up (an old Beetle from
the sixties, rust rimming the headlights, a guy's square
face over the leather steering wheel) there was this
confused little dance of him moving toward the car
and me trying to anticipate his moves so I could get
out of his way, and his lower arm brushed against
mine, right near our wrists, our veins so close to the
surface, *touching* there too.

It was like being burned. A current travelled
through those veins, and the heat radiated outward,
my skin inflamed from the inside. As I caught Ian's
glance, I had to wonder if he felt it too since he seemed
to hang in the air, like me. Then he made the decision
to cup my left elbow in his hand and say:

"Guess I'll see you at the city finals."

He was nonchalant, crossing to the other side to
get in the car. I peered into the car's interior, hoping I
wasn't making it obvious. Was there the hint of a smile
on his lips when his slack-jawed buddy mouthed,
"Who was that?" when I watched him answer with a
simple shrug of his shoulders?

My insides were quivering, but on the outside I
managed a "yes!" that sounded like a desperate squeal
(I punished myself for that the rest of the night—
"Stupid. *Stoopid*!") and focused all my energy on
walking normally, looking as normal as possible.

Sure, I could look over my shoulder. Looking once
is okay, right? I caught his buddy putting the car in

drive. Were they going to drive past me? Can I look twice? Naw, the guy's doing a three-point turn to go the other way down the street. But Ian was looking my way, right? I could look a third time. No, forget it. Out of the question.

The car's taillights glowed red briefly at the corner before disappearing down Main, *his* touch still radiating fire up my arm.

I kept it together down the block, but once I got to the corner, I sprinted, like a happy freak, down the labyrinth of streets, all the way home. It took a couple of tries with the key I'd used before I finally slammed through the door, pounded up the stairs and vaulted onto my bed, nearly crashing into the wall.

I giggled and wriggled down onto the mattress, plugging in my headphones and listening to music until the early morning, the lights of the nearby apartment towers lighting my window as I vibrated in the darkness.

Of course I woke up this morning with a huge case of the guilts, not only for remembering that I helped get Alicia grounded, but also that I went to the dance I said I wouldn't help her go to even though she wanted it so much more than I did. *And* I *connected* with R.S.

It's funny how things change. Because right now, with that March wind creeping up inside my jacket, I treasure that memory. Instead of mourning the death of the most solid friendship I've ever had, I wrap that memory around me and use it to keep me warm.

#14
i hate march

I hate March. The second week in March was when Girl #1 was taken. March and October were the months when the bad men take off the masks that are their everyday faces and set them beside their alarm clocks on the side table, throw them beside the empties lying on the floor, or hide them under their pillow beside their sleeping girlfriends, and comb the city to look for us: the little girls, the big girls. Girls like me.

Do I know Faceless Man is out to get me? Maybe he's just a guy new to the city, lost, like I thought Taxi Man was. But if Faceless Man was a nice guy wouldn't he, witnessing my freak-out behind the evergreen, have said something like, "Oops, I'm sorry I scared you. I'm looking for such-and-such a crescent?" Like harmless Mildred and Hal who just went away.

I know he's a bad man—aside from the creepy lack of facial features, at least in my fevered eyes—because he didn't just *not* go away, he followed me into the ravine, and into this forest. A forest in *my* ravine. The one with secrets, just like me, the one with The Hornet's Nest.

At least I still have an advantage over him. On a normal day I'd avoid this particular place like the plague. But today it's not evil. It's comforting. It's not back-of-my-hand familiar like the other nooks and crannies in my woods, but I still know it. I was here once. On a bad night.

I hear the squish of his boots on the muddy path. Stop. Then *squish-squish*-stop. Even though I'm squirreled away in my Supreme Hiding Place near the Hornet's Nest, I'm not confident enough to stick my neck out and take a look around. In the movies, that's when people get shot in the head.

I can only imagine him looking up at the umbrella of oak trees and down the crooked mud path that leads to the clearing below. Search and destroy . . .

"Excuse me?"

His voice is boyish and edged with irritation. The trees swallow his words immediately after he says them. That could be the tagline for a slash flick: In the forest, no one can hear you scream! He coughs then puts on a fake calm voice.

"I'm sorry if I startled you. I didn't mean to." He pauses, "Hello? Hello?"

Like I'm so stupid I'm going to pop out and wave.

Here I am, Faceless Man. Are you lost? No, oh, okay, just forget you saw me, okay?

Faceless Man is still talking, over the monologue in my head.

"Are you hurt? It's alright. I just wanted to ask you something. It's okay."

Liar, liar! Just like Matt in the Hornet's Nest, moving his hands: ugh, revulsion. But then I recall the sensation of Ian's accidental touch, the sweet warmth that spreads from it. Like a cocoon. Like something to look forward to.

Don't let your guard down.

Faceless Man's touch would feel like this: clammy, dead, death.

He's still talking, his deceptively sweet voice bouncing off the tree trunks. "So I was wondering if you saw this person I know. He drives a taxi?"

So that's it. The mention of Taxi Man unsettles me. It is an interesting twist, more original than the "I was lost" line. And don't even ask me how he can talk without a mouth.

He's not going to go away unless he kills me, right?

You saw his face. You have a description you can pass on to the police.

But he doesn't have a face!

Exactly. And who in the world would believe that?

My whole being trembles. I clutch the tree. The trunk scratches my already numb hands, my fingernails ringed with mud.

Remember, no sudden moves. He isn't gonna find

you if you don't move. It's not like he can hear your thoughts, right?

Faceless Man's on the move again. I hear his boots *squish-squish-squish* as he continues to scan the bush, calling out cautiously "Hello?"

I peer around the tree. He's about twenty feet away and has my windbreaker in his hands. The sight of Faceless Man pawing a personal possession of mine unleashes another wave of nausea mixed with anger. I had to sacrifice it; its red sheen was what gave me away behind the gnarled hedge. The fact that Faceless Man has quietly consumed it and continued his silent prowl down the path proves to me, once again, that he is a bad man. A good man would've called out, "Hey, you must've dropped your jacket! I'll leave it for you and go, okay? Sorry to scare you!" Like I said, a good man wouldn't have followed me down into the ravine either.

Keep going down the path, buddy, I mutter to myself. Keep on going, so I can come out of my hiding place, so I can race away from you, so I can go home. Crap! I remember my cart and my remaining papers. I mean, so I can go home after I do those last three papers. Once a papergirl, always a papergirl. It's part of my identity. Without it and track and Ripley, I'm nothing, a nameless spot for Faceless Man to blot out. I grasp the tree with my free arm to feel something tangible—rough bark grates my right cheek.

Then Faceless Man does something crazy. Instead

of continuing down the main path toward the clearing, he veers to the right, finding a small break in the bush. He wraps my windbreaker around his legs like a shield and dives in, the thorns grating their high-pitch complaint on the nylon instead of poking through his jeans. He's heading into the Hornet's Nest, a clearing of bush walled in by thorn bushes. A head of red flashes above the nest before it ducks down to safety. Faceless Man is drawn to it like a flame. It doesn't matter that it's not my hair colour. He slows to a prowl. He's at the mouth of the nest. He peers over the edge, hoping to find me, but I'm not there.

Faceless Man and I aren't alone in this forest anymore. Girl #2 is here too. She was the one who pointed out this Supreme Hiding Space. She didn't point exactly, that's far too obvious. She merely stood by it, giving me her placid look. Strangely, I've gotten used to her presence now, how she can disappear and reappear at will. For a while she was in the Hornet's Nest, as if she was leading Faceless Man away from me. But now, in a blink, she's reappeared at the mouth of the nest staring dispassionately at him as he burrows through its overgrown maze.

He can't see her—that much is clear. It's not like he would care anyway. She's dead and he's focused on one thing: finding me. Stupid man, I've already been led into the Hornet's Nest once. You think I'd go in there a second time? Of course, he doesn't know things like that about me. Or does he?

I can't see him from my Supreme Hiding Place but I hear the squish of his boots. Girl #2 watches too, her head turned his way. For one crazy minute, I wish I could switch bodies with her, if what she currently occupies could be described as a body. She can go any-where undetected. She can't get hurt, unlike me. I can't risk moving until he leaves. Jesus God, just hurry and leave! The morning wind hasn't subsided and the cold shakes me. My teeth chatter as I attempt to meld my stubby body in with the elements.

I'm hidden. Go away!

I hear a car's motor on Ravine Ridge. I look through the gnarled canopy of branches: a bright sky peaks through. It's probably close to 9 a.m. now. My time is almost up—only a half-hour to get ready for the rehearsal. Good thing Faceless Man's time is also almost up. It's a little hard to abduct girls when the neighbourhood is waking up and suddenly you have witnesses.

Girl #2's ghost or whatever she is must be curious to find out what's up with Faceless Man because she suddenly turns and enters the nest after him, not mak-ing a sound. Her pale form is more translucent in the growing heat of the day. Deep in the nest, I hear more *snap-crackle-pops* from Faceless Man, even a few curses.

My hands, already rubbed raw, tremble violently. I wedge my right-hand fingers deeper into the bark's crevices until I sense blood circulation halting. I imagine the tips turning as brown as the tree trunk, which just provides improved camouflage anyway. My other hand has fallen asleep under a dead grey weight. Occasionally the crushed nerves shoot out an electric jolt to remind me that my left hand hasn't fallen off yet, but it's not like I could release it from its sentence. That'd give away everything. I send Girl #2 a mental message:

Please, get rid of him. Make him see you and scare him away. I gotta go home. Let me go home.

I don't know if she can read my thoughts or what, but with a final, scrapping rustle, Faceless Man emerges from the nest. I could shriek with joy, except the sight of his wooden, carved face fills me with dread—the familiar ice water returns to cascade through my veins.

Girl #2 has reappeared. Though now she's standing below us on the west slope, the one with the path that leads down further into the ravine. She's still regarding Faceless Man with that weirdly calm gaze as he takes one last survey of the forest around him. I hold my breath. The ice water sloshing in my belly is quickly sucking all remaining heat from my body. You could hear my teeth chattering from the highway, my heart races like wild horses and my hands shake so bad I'm afraid I'm going to fall right on him.

I pray: Just don't look up.

Did I say that out loud? I could have sworn that I didn't, but why is Faceless Man suddenly *looking up*?

And how can he see *anything* out of those hollow eyes? But that's exactly what he's done. He's zeroed in on my Supreme Hiding Place—the arms of the oak tree above the Hornet's Nest. I managed to scramble up into its branches before he caught up to me.

I'm dead. The wind cuts through my chest cavity and I shudder a sob. I'm going to die in this ravine— *my* ravine—like the others. I can't even see Girl #2's shadow flitting in and out of sight—that is, if I really saw her in the first place.

And suddenly Faceless Man has a mouth of flesh complete with lush lips. When the frig did he grow a mouth? And he grins wide and he speaks, still polite, with only a trace of gloating:

"What are you doing up there?" he cajoles, like I'm a wayward kitten that won't come down for the fireman.

It's not only his mouth that's newly formed. Most of Faceless Man's face is flesh now. There's a bump on his nose like it was once broken, there's a soft cleft to his chin, a scar on his cheek, but his eyes—they're still empty wood sockets. I'd be too terrified to see what his real eyes looked like. He keeps talking in this infuriatingly calm voice like he has all the time in the world. And in my case it's not true what they say: you *don't* always know your killer.

"What did you mean by you know about me?"

I give away nothing. I attempt to memorize every fresh curve of Faceless Man's emerging face.

"Did a cabbie tell you something about me?" he asks soberly.

I barely nod.

"He's a liar," Faceless Man says crisply. And to prove it he gives me a grin, newly formed, showing beautiful square teeth, too—pearly, not wooden, like real humans. "I apologize if he scared you."

He's smooth, this guy. He doesn't think I notice him assessing the lower branches of the tree, of which there are few—the knolls in the trunk that I used as steps when I scurried up. Faceless Man's wondering if he could climb up if I won't come down.

"Did you understand what I said?"

I give a curt nod.

"Now what are you still doing up there?" smiles No Eyes Man.

It's then that No Eyes Man places a lean hand on the tree, *my* tree. His fingers are long and elegant, the kind that might have a Rolex at the wrist end of them. His casualness pisses me off. You can do this, I think. Sure, to him I look like a shivering mouse with chapped hands and bloody lines cutting my face, but he doesn't know me. He doesn't have a clue.

"You know," he continues. "I know you're a girl who likes to have some fun. You were out late last night, right? Out with a boy? Maybe an older boy?" The grin. "Does your mother know?"

My insides are beyond ice water.

He pats the tree. "Why don't you just come down?

You don't want any trouble, do you?"

With a shaky hand, I produce the boulder I've been balancing on my knee this whole time. My fingers have long since melded into the stone's eternal cold. Just the act of outstretching my arm burns my rigid muscles. Turning my hand over, releasing the weight is a relief.

The boulder lands on target, but instead of the hollow *crack* of his wooden head, I hear a sloppy thud, like a watermelon thrown from a window.

I cling to the tree. With every breath, my expanded chest forces my cheek to scrape against another crevice in my tree, but I'm past caring. My lips and cheek are numbed in this frigid air and I'm not leaving this tree. I start counting.

Blood seeps from his temple onto the dead leaves, small and round like a thought bubble.

"... *fifteen, sixteen, seventeen* ..."

The bubble expands. It coats the fallen leaves as if a can of paint broke open on the ground and No Eyes Man decided to dive headfirst into the puddle.

"... *twenty-nine, thirty, thirty-one* ..."

He shudders. I stop counting. I stop breathing. The good thing is by not inhaling, I also stop ravaging my cheek on the tree bark.

I'm dizzy. No Eyes Man relaxes in his unconscious position. Maybe, just maybe, I could slide down. While he's down. Maybe.

Then behind me whooshes the ghost of Girl #2,

her red hair a flag sailing up the hill to the street above. She carries with her one message, a whisper:

Get out of here.

I aim for the ground. I hear a rip as my track pant leg catches on the nub of a branch, feel wetness on my skin. But by then I'm pretending that I've just come off the curve for the final hundred-metre stretch. My legs are sand bags, my lungs empty canisters, but it's the fire in my belly that keeps my arms and legs pumping. That's the trick of the 400 metres—it's a brutally long sprint. When your body begins to cry in agony, that's when you have to turn your mind off, you have to push past the pain and let the euphoria carry you over the finish line, where you can finally stop—you can fall in a heap, muscles deflated, energy spent, liquid streaming from your nose, your mouth, your open eyes registering relief.

Only afterwards, once you've recovered, do you realize that it seemed way too easy.

3

a second visit

#15
Home

I'm on fire: my palms, my legs, my brain. You won't believe this, but yesiree, professional to the point of death, literally, I did those last papers in record time, flying past the first dog walkers on the street. I rescued my windbreaker (don't think about touching his flesh), my cart and my bike all where they had fallen, and now I'm flashing down Pine, down Main, careful to turn my face when I pass the odd sleepwalking human so they can't stare at the flaming scratches on my face, see the blood on my hands. I pump adrenaline all the way home.

I did it! I was smarter than he was. I can see my house up ahead.

I made it home!

Still, Mum should be wide awake and if she's in new psycho mode then she could be standing on our porch waiting to blow. I ease up on the speed and bike Ripley beside a line of parked minivans and wagons, ducking my head low. Peering through the smoked windows of our next-door neighbour's bone-white minivan, I see no sign of Mum. Score!

I race up the driveway and flip open the garage door to lock Ripley up. Strange, in the garage, there's no sign of our car either. This is bad. Just get in the house, I command myself. I take the safe entrance through the laundry room.

"Mum!" I call out in a stupid perky voice.

There's no response. I catch the time on the clock on the stove: nine twenty-five. Uh-oh. Did she leave early? I pummel up the stairs and slam the door to the bathroom. I crank the taps until the pipes squeal. The voice in my head argues with me.

You're toast! Your mum already left for the rehearsal and when she comes back, she'll skin you alive.

That would be a better fate than wearing the peach dress and who cares? I beat him! I beat No Eyes Man!

I want to scream it so everyone in the neighbourhood can hear. Instead, my naked feet beat a victory dance in the shower. The hot water streams through my spiky hair and warms my skin still numb from the March air. I crank up the water temperature until the tiny bathroom fills with steam. Soon my skin will be on fire like the rest of me. I bunch a ratty washcloth and scour the dirt from the creases in my hands, squeeze warmth between my soft, pudgy toes.

I check out my handiwork in the steamed-up

mirror afterward, standing naked on the fluffy terry mat, my skin rubbed a raw pink. The scratches on my face and hands stand out like lesions. I marvel at their exclamations, my battle scars. My eyes are wild like an animal's. I could dive into the black pools of my pupils. The look they send back both enthrals and unnerves me.

"It's okay," I tell the mirror. "You're safe. You're *home!*"

Then why does it feel like I'm still being chased?

I shake that nasty thought off like a chill on my shoulders, but the cold continues to sink in.

You know you did say you'd call the police, ventures Bossy Voice, sounding more like my reluctant Responsible voice.

I didn't promise that, did I?

'Fraid so—you were crouched behind that pathetic excuse of a bush. Also, up in the tree. You said it a couple times.

I'm pretty sure my heart has now stopped. My blood has stopped moving. It's—what's the word?— coagulating in my veins. The air's stopped moving too. Maybe I'll suffocate standing still grasping for a response. One comes.

I have to get ready first. Imagine if Mum shows and she sees my arms and face with, like, thrasher scratches right before the rehearsal? She'll super-freak.

Responsible Voice murmurs.

If I'm not ready when and if Mum comes home,

it's all over. You know that. I might as well move out now.

I guess . . . , trails off Responsible Voice. "Guess" comes in two long syllables.

Decided—camouflage first, call police later.

My heart restarts. So do my lungs. I wrap my body in a towel and creep into Mum's bedroom, half-expecting to barge in on her sitting at her glass makeup table, applying a fan of black-widow eyeliner for the umpteenth time. Except she's still gone; in the quiet, my heart thumps on my freshly cleaned skin.

Maybe she just ran an errand and she's coming back—soon. If so, I better get in gear.

There are so many carefully lined jars on her counter it's impossible to know where to start. So I just pick one. The gunk inside is light beige: I guess this is what they call "foundation." I mop it onto my face and on my hands until it disguises all cuts and scratches, but now I look like the living dead. I dully remember then reject the makeup conventions Alicia raves about reading in airhead fashion mags. I powder too much "Delicious Berry" on my cheeks, paint my lips "Deep Aubergine," and rim my eyes in "Bright Peacock" to punch out my panic, my victory. When I'm done my face is a riot of colour, each feature screaming for attention—not bad for a first timer!

Now I have to put the jars back. There's no way I can remember which went where, so I shove them in a line and make haste to my room. I'm wondering where the heck Mum is when my cell starts playing my song—the annoying ditty I have it programmed to when only Mum calls.

It's calling from the couch cushions. In the living room. Great. I let it play its three chords and hear its loud shriek indicating that I have a message. I creep downstairs and pick up the cell like it's a bomb. The number was coming from Mum's cell, which means she's on the road. I check my messages: three voice mails from Mum—I delete them—and one text from Alicia that I read.

"herd u wento danc ..."

Oh great. Like I can deal with this right now. Does she know I talked to Ian? I mean, I just talked to him. I didn't even *do* anything with Ian, I argue to an imaginary jury of peers. Besides, it's her own fault for lying to her parents and getting grounded. Otherwise, she could've gone to the dance herself—harsh, but true. And, wait a minute, how the hell did she even know I went?

My head throbs with too many questions. I sit on the edge of my bed to steady myself. The makeup itches my skin and adds to my growing panic. A breeze blows in from the window and with it, a whisper:

Maybe, while you're waiting, you could make a phone call ...

This is annoying. Why would I do that *now*?

Because you know it's not like that body is going to stay hidden in the Hornet's Nest forever.

The panic under my skin takes a leap.

Someone will find him. That is, if he's actually dead in the first place.

Wait, I didn't kill anyone! It was self-defence. It's done. The cycle is over.

Not if he gets up.

The white towel wrapped around my body may be plush, but a chill sluices through it to my bones.

Make it anonymous. You can put on another track suit, bike up to the plaza, call from a pay phone.

It's impossibly frigid inside my bedroom.

And why don't I tell them that the ghost of a dead girl helped me out, too?

Sarcasm shuts the voice up.

My watch flashes nine forty-five. No way. I can't go. If Mum comes back and I'm not here, I'm dead. We'd be late for the rehearsal and she'd freak.

Still, if there was anytime to go, it would be now. Maybe Mum did go without me. But I can't do it. I can't do anything because while I've been listening and arguing with crazy-sane voice, the front door has opened with an unmistakeable thunder.

"Sidonia!"

Yup, Psycho Mum has returned to her roost. The house shakes with: "I thought you were *dead*!"

Imagine the inconvenience.

The house does not stop shaking until well after we leave. Mum rags about spilled makeup jars, derailed schedules, and speedily packs her baby girl, me, in peach, but not before pocketing my cellphone—"*This was a useful investment*"—while nearly suffocating me with a towel before dropping the dress over my head to protect it from my day-glo makeup experiment, didn't you know, which she then blots into subtler shades with a facecloth like I'm two and have my supper smeared all over my face.

Oh yeah—she noticed my battle scars during the facecloth cleanup.

"I'm not even going to *ask* how you got those. The things you do for amusement, I can't imagine." The accusations drip as does the concealer. I'm a chewed thigh bone, stripped of its meat, mute and dolled up in a pretty dress.

Just let her have her way and you will get through this.

We hit the road in less than ten minutes.

Bossy Voice whispers her apologies after I slip numbly into the passenger seat: *Wow, can you imagine if a cop had reacted like that? To have that come from a stranger? That would be a million times worse.*

When the dress rehearsal is over, I'll get my life back. When it's over, I'll figure out what to do.

#16,
dress rehearsal

"I looked for you for an hour, Sidonia," Mum chides. "Where were you?"

I'm in the car. I'm in the dress. We're hurtling down the 401 in the company of Saturday mall shoppers. Maybe we'll hit a guard rail before we get to Islington. Wouldn't that be ironic: I escaped No Eyes Man only to end up as a highway statistic.

I mutter into my neck something about doing papers. I run fidgety fingers over the atrocious Hello Kitty bridesmaid purse, a dead weight in my lap.

"But I didn't see you *at all*, Sidonia. There was no sign of your cart, no sign of your bike . . ."

Ripley is her name, I think back at her as I fidget. The multi-beads on the purse are making my fingers oily.

". . . there was no sign of *anyone*. It was as if you had disappeared *entirely* from the street."

At least I had fooled my mother. If only No Eyes Man had been so easily misled. I contemplate asking her if she, by chance, had seen a car parked on the street, a white car. Maybe she caught a licence plate number? Maybe she saw a man and he had real features—like a crooked nose or a ripping scar across his cheek or two legs of different lengths, an obvious limp—some notable description to give to the cops that would *corroborate* my little nightmare?

I bite my tongue to stop these questions from flowing. I don't need to give Mum any more ammo to conduct an inquisition. What I need is for her to stop harassing me.

We turn off the highway onto Islington, continuing south, then zigzag down a series of unfamiliar side streets filled with bungalows and high fences. Mum's still muttering about my disappearing act, but I've tuned her out, head resting on the window. The pulse in my temple pounds on glass.

Don't think about No Eyes Man lying facedown in the park! Don't think about No Eyes Man lying facedown in the park! Think of R.S., think of his touch.

It isn't working. I squirm in the seat and stare outside. We drive by a parkette where kids are running around in T-shirts and light sweaters. I may be numb and shivering under my silk inside Mum's car, but outside the world is suddenly warming. As we drive by, I see a flash of long, black pigtails behind a swing set. My heart lunges—Girl #1? What is she doing in this neighbourhood so far west from where she lived and where she was found? And now I'm seeing *two* ghosts?

I take another look. God, I'm going manic. I feel dizzy, my mouth runs dry.

The girl, who is definitely not a ghost, looks nothing like Girl #1. In fact, her black pigtails are actually a Scandinavian cap with knitted braids that knock along the side of her face. She is pushing a young boy who looks about five on the adult swings. No, it couldn't be Girl #1. She was the youngest of three girls; there was no younger brother.

I must be certifiable. But the mistaken sighting kick-starts my blood. As we pass by a mini forest, I might as well be back in the high branches of the scratchy oak tree staring down into Faceless Man's eyes, because suddenly I remember—he finally grew eyes at the precise moment the boulder crashed into his front lobe. His eyes were so pale they disappeared into the whites around them and now they appear, blinking, in the folds of my peach dress. I jump. A groan escapes from my lips. It was an *accident!*

Was it really?

"What's the matter with you?" Mum freaks.

"Dad isn't going to be there, right?" My shriek rings in my ears before I've realized what I said.

Mum is stunned into silence. She veers quickly to the side of the road, parks by another stretch of mute bungalows, motor still running, and contemplates the steering wheel. Meanwhile my heart has jumped out of my chest and is running down the road. I'd claw at the ceiling if I had nails.

Mum chooses her words carefully. "Why would you say that, Sidonia?"

"Because I won't be able to take it if he's just going to show up! I can't handle it."

I'm hyperventilating now, acutely aware how cramped it is in the car, the sun beating its warmth on the window, the air inside expanding like rising dough, suffocating me.

"No," Mum says finally. Her words are as hollow as the air. "Why would he? It's only a rehearsal."

Another lie: I've heard her phone conversations with The Bride, I know something is up. Maybe it's only in Mum's head but it's a possibility. Even the way she's gnawing ever so slightly on her bottom lip as she puts the car in drive and steers it back into the street— *think of the matte lipstick! Oh, the carnage*—I know that the concept of Dad showing is eating away at her. Instead, she covers up and lies. Why can't she *ever* be straight with me? When it comes to me, she glosses over everything that's bad in the world.

Example: One morning, Mum catches me reading a newspaper that just happens to have a cover story about Girl #1.

"This is why young people shouldn't read the news, Sidonia," she said as she plucked away my copy. "It will only upset you."

I wasn't even reading the story, but she managed to get up earlier than me for the next couple of weeks and squirrel away all the front pages before I had a chance to read them. I had to check the cover story out at school, on the Internet, grab a free issue at the library, copy it, study the details, figure how to avoid ending up like her—drawn to her stats like a gawker to a car wreck.

Example: Matt the Freak leaving creepo messages on my cellphone last fall.

"Boys just want attention and sometimes they can't express themselves properly," she said, in response to my blubbering confession (that was hard enough for me in the first place, without having to hear her trivialize it!).

Example: Faceless Man forcing me to take cover behind a car, in a bush, in a tree.

"What were you doing this morning: playing in the ravine?" She's like a broken record. The problem's always me. "Did you run off to the smoke shop? I even went up to a few of the houses, Sidonia. I found copies of *The Carrier* in their mailbox. You had already delivered your papers, so where were you?"

Stalked by my own mother. She and Faceless Man could've had coffee.

I clutch my dress with both fists without realizing it, I swear. Then I hope, sadistically, that the combo of sweat and makeup that is now melting off me—the angry red scrapes on my hands re-emerging—will have maximum stain impact.

When we arrive at St. George's Anglican, I'm in full-panic mode. Mum parks, hesitates, then tentatively pats my shoulder.

"Everything will be fine," she says unconvincingly.

My lungs have stopped working. The interior of the car buckles and bloats, the glove compartment dissolves into a million yellow stars. My stomach swells with unreleased air.

"I'm going to throw up!" I blurt out. "I'm going to do it right here in the car, I swear."

"Don't be silly, Sidonia," Mum says. Except this time there's a note of sympathy in her voice. I dully think playing the "Dad card" was the right thing to do. Distract her. Maybe even get me out of this sham of a wedding rehearsal? "We can skip the lunch afterward if you aren't feeling well, but you have to do this. Let's go."

Game over. My heels dig into the loose gravel in the parking lot. I follow Mum, like a sick sheep, into the church, careful not to look into the dark woods that surround the back of the church lot so I don't see a flash of a wooden face, a streak of red hair.

St. George's is one of those churches that must have been built in horse-and-buggy times, when the only people living out in Etobicoke were pioneers who wore hankies and hats on their heads and were constantly covered in dirt. The church entrance is cramped and dark, and its haunted floors creak.

Mum hooks her arm into mine and forces, I mean, *encourages* me forward as we walk under tattered

Union Jacks and dusty versions of Canada's old flag hanging from the ceiling like forgotten boughs of holly. I focus my eyes on the tight toes of my shoes to avoid all dark corners. Nice! I'm already starting to get a red cut line on my fat big toe where it squishes out the teeny opening of my shoes, cutting off circulation. This better not affect my training schedule.

Mum pulls me around a corner and my eyes wince at a bright blast of light. The congregation hall is distractingly light thanks to a spanking new bank of picture windows overlooking the thick forest outside. It makes me wonder why anyone would close their eyes to pray when you had this view, much less listen to a minister drone on.

Then, we're assaulted by The Bride, who jumps out from behind a pew.

Okay, first, I should say that Mum's cousin Ally-Maude, a.k.a. "The Bride," is probably the nicest person in Mum's stuck-up family. Unfortunately, it's an intense sugar-rush kind of nice.

"*Sidonia*!" she squeals, three inches from my face, squeezing my hands like rubber balls. "You look like such a *woman*! Hee!"

Light spit peppers my face. All I see is purple gums, gnashing teeth, and skin as tight as stuffed knackwurst. The water in my stomach sloshes as The Bride manages to invade my personal space further.

"Now I have to introduce you to your *usher*!" she whispers.

I'm in a game show from hell and The Bride is the hostess. I throw a panicked look to Mum, who is wearing one of her inscrutable "I'm-not-going-to-save-you" smiles as Ally-Maude drags me up the aisle.

Of course, The Bride is not wearing the big white dress—she has some kind of white tracksuit-pantsuit-thing on. Only the gaggle of bridesmaids and ushers stuck in a mid-range pew are in their beaded peach silks and their brown clown suits, "to get the true effect," says A-M. We arrive at the wedding crew.

My usher—I've already seen his name in swirled script on the wedding program. Darek with an "a"; maybe he's a cool individual or maybe his name was just a typo and he's plain old Derek. I quickly scan the group, suddenly hopeful for an Ian-look-alike who will emerge and calm me with a quiet confidence. Instead, The Bride plucks out a freakishly tall guy with skin the colour of translucent stone and a mop of brown hair hiding most of his face and thrusts him my way.

"*This* is *Darek*!" The Bride says, like we've been paired up since birth.

Darek is in grade twelve. I guess he's attractive in a kind of underfed rock star way, *except* for the black bush of hairs sticking out of his nose. And he's clearly not impressed he got stuck with "the kid." He grunts something approximating a hi then continues to look longingly at a perky bridesmaid who clearly didn't need to have her bust line taken in. Ally-Maude catches me looking.

"That's Stacie! She's only sixteen. Can you believe it?" she squeals. She goes on to tell me Stacie does catalogue work for Sears, but all I can think of is how she's obviously flirting with her usher, whose beard is climbing up his face and who looks old enough to be her dad.

So my usher's no Ian. In a way I'm glad. This means I can ignore him and not feel guilty. All I have to do is walk up this stupid aisle with him, stand at the front of the church, nod my head at instructions, walk back, then I'm done. That'll take, what, fifteen minutes tops? I grease a wet palm along the beads on my Hello Kitty clutch purse.

Psst! No one is going to find the body.

"It was an accident," I whisper. Or self-defence, maybe.

I toss the purse from palm to palm. It's a slippery eel in my hands.

Don't think about Faceless Man. Don't wipe your hands on your dress. Pretend your stomach isn't churning.

A-M herds us to the back of the church where I join the other sheep. We pass by Mum sitting in a back pew, face turned to the bank of windows, warmed by the rising noon sun. It may soon be spring after all. I wonder about Faceless Man facedown in the leaves. Maybe if it gets warmer, he'll wake up. Maybe if it gets warmer, more people—kids, families, dog walkers—will head to the ravine and trip over him. Maybe they'll ask questions about who on Earth would be up and around early that Saturday morning. Did they see anyone suspicious? Anyone who looked like a killer?

An unseen fist clenches around my intestines.

Self-defence. It definitely was that.

Better not look at the window. Stare at the tip of your shoe and the unnatural way your big toe is bulging out of the tip, feel the blisters form. My big toe is being crushed by the slowest-pinching crab claw in the world and is now a fabulous shade of indigo.

Just breathe.

A-M guides the first couple down the aisle: the "Best Lady and Man," who are near clones of The Bride and Groom—middle aged, chunky, and ridiculously chirpy. They are followed by a moping couple of dark cousins who are maybe thirty, then Stacie and her flirty "daddy" usher (eww).

Darek's been fiddling with his bangs the entire time we've been waiting our turn at the back of the church. Once he thinks his bangs are perfectly arranged, he tilts his head at this stupid angle to make sure his hair hangs in his face correctly. But "perfect" doesn't last long. Then he has to start from scratch.

I can't stop gawking at the whole process—it's so bizarre seeing a guy fuss over his hair—and Darek can't stop staring at Stacie's butt. I know he's thinking about it because sweat's trickling down his nose past the black bush jutting out from it.

This is good. Focusing on Darek's hair issues is

making me forget about Faceless Man (almost) completely. The knot in my belly relaxes.

From her conductor's pit at the head of the church, A-M gives me and Darek the nod. We waltz, my toe wails in pain. The fresh blisters are going to explode their sticky clear liquid in my shoe. But A-M is yelling from the nave:

"No, no! *Slow.* With *grace.* Pause after each step."

So, I pause, grimace-smile, step, and peer at Darek's massive nose-bush for distraction. I can't believe A-M will let that hairy monster appear in her wedding photos. Maybe, once Darek and I get to the front of the church, she'll freak, whip a weed-whacker out of her pantsuit, and go to town.

I giggle. Darek gives me a sharp look, causing his hair to fall off his face in the wrong way, which gets him really mad. His fingers start flipping and my giggles become choked belly laughs.

"Immature," Darek mutters.

We continue walking.

Step—toe screams in pain—a popped blister! Liquid excretes into my shoe—grimace-smile—pause.

Except now I'm shaking so hard with inner laughter, I might just pee. I bite my lip and look out the bank of windows. There's a flash of a girl running in front of the woods, her red hair a flag. It ices my laughter.

"God, you're bleeding," Darek groans.

What's *that* supposed to mean? And what kind of

thing is that to tell a girl anyway! The unseen fist twists at my guts again.

No, there is *no flash* of red hair! Girl #2 has not followed you to the church! Darek's just a big jerk.

I hiss to Darek, "You've got boogers hanging from your nose hairs—green goobery grapes!"

His look of horror and frantic motions are almost worth the price of admission to this wedding party. Darek cups his nose and wipes whatever greasy grime he catches from his nostrils on the thighs of his beige suit pants. He repeats this about twenty times. A-M spies this and runs toward us down the aisle. Score! My usher's going to get ejected for using his rental suit as a snot rag!

Except A-M isn't coming to ream out Darek, she's jabbering and pointing at me, at my shoe. Soon, both she and Mum have surrounded me, eyes directed to the ground.

It wasn't a blister that burst; the stupid shoe cut a semi-circle into my big toe, which is now burbling blood over the nice beige two-hundred-dollar leather. A flash of Faceless Man's bloody thought bubble appears in the aisle and I furiously blink the image away.

The Bride's jabbering about expensive Bata shoes, Mum soothingly describes club soda as a solution to remove any stain. I'm angry—now *this* is going to affect my training.

#17
a visitation

The church bathroom is a tiny, dank water closet in the basement, but at least it keeps Mum outside, meekly knocking on the door.

"How is it?" She sounds so neutral, so unlike her freaked-out self this morning.

I've hoisted my leg up so my naked foot rests in the sink. Cold tap water runs the blood off my cut and the remaining makeup off my hands. The scrapes from this morning's battle resurface.

"I won't be able to walk," I yell through the door.

Mum exhales an "okay" like a drag on a cigarette. That was easy, dare I hope?

"Mum," I caution, "I think I should go home."

"Yes," she agrees. "I forget how weddings depress me." She taps a circle on the linoleum floor before adding: "I'll be outside having a smoke." Her heels snap and click decisively down the hall and up the stairs.

I'd do a victory dance except my foot is still hanging

over the sink. Water droplets splash over my dress, but who cares? I'm heading home! Maybe I'll call Alicia and tell her I'm sorry I went to the dance, but I met Ian, but whatever, it's cool if she still likes him and all. I'll back off. Maybe I'll even be too wounded to hobble down the aisle with Booger Face tomorrow, but maybe that's too much to hope for.

Then there's the other thing I should check on.

Don't think about it! commands Bossy Voice. *Just get outta here.*

Don't think. I dry my foot with sandpaper towels, stuff a wad of toilet paper into the toe of my shoe and brace myself before jamming my foot in. Only a dull pain reverberates in my foot before it numbs to an ache. I do a hobble-walk upstairs and lean against the barred door to the parking lot, watching Mum smoke outside through the little window.

Did I mention that the old part of this church creeps me out? It's all dark corners and ancient flags wafting thanks to unseen hands, and there's this constant draft blowing the hairs on my neck. Windows the size of playing cards let dusty light through the parking-lot door, which I lean my back against. It's metal and soothing. Mum's cigarette smoke curls under the rubber seal of the door to tickle my nose hairs. It's so quiet in this mouse corner, I should be relaxed, but my heart is pumping like it did in the ravine.

Faceless Man is *dead* and that's a good thing

because he can't collect any more girls. He can't collect *me*.

My blood pounds louder in my ears.

Faceless Man is *not* dead and that's a good thing because it means I didn't murder anyone. No blood on my hands, only in my shoe.

I squeeze tears out of my eyes.

Bossy Voice coos to me: *Just wait here until your Mum finishes her butt. Then you can go home, safe home.*

Except maybe Faceless Man is waiting for me there?

Maybe he dusted himself off the minute I ran past the edge of the still-skeletal forest and over the hill, safely out of view. Maybe he got back into his car and trailed me home. Maybe he waited under the over-grown oak tree with its precarious hanging branches two doors down and scoped out the house, not quite sure if I was home or not. But then a car drove up and Mum, in her new-robot mode popped out and soon whisked me off, silk dress and all. And he's still there, waiting. Maybe I don't know him, but maybe he knows me. Maybe he's been following me on my route, hovering outside my house for weeks, months.

He knew I went to the dance last night.

My heart is outracing a squirrel on speed but I can't stop this movie from playing.

Even Bossy Voice concedes: *Okay, maybe Faceless Man's followed you here and is waiting for you in the parking lot, in the shade of trees that you know wind their way behind bland subdivisions until they join their brothers in the Humber Valley, the second ravine. Maybe he's waiting behind this very door. Anything's possible, I guess.*

I've stopped breathing. I'm so freaked out by this point that I can't move. My back is fused to the door; its cool metal has permeated my spine. So when it opens, I fall in slow motion, just like they do in the movies. My knees buckle, my butt sticks out. I'll probably crack my spine on the concrete step behind me. Yep, there goes my running, I think dully, but there's no way I can stop this motion; at this point, I can't stop anything. Just bring it on.

But before my tailbone hits the ground, the bend of my back hits something soft but solid. A hand—a man's wide, warm hand—cups my right elbow, the other catches me under my left arm. Anonymous fingers narrowly miss the tiny bump that is my left breast. I hang in his arms, paralyzed.

Only this warm body doesn't smell like the ravine—more like sickly peppery cinnamon, but that doesn't mean anything. Faceless Man could have followed me here. It's all I can do to force my neck to turn upward and look into his face.

But it isn't Faceless Man. The man's face—handsome, familiar, backlit by the sun—belongs to my Dad.

#18
Him

For a split second, I think he is a ghost. Is there a limit to how many ghosts you can see in a day? Probably not; probably the minute you start seeing ghosts in the plural, you should sign yourself into the nearest loony bin.

But ghosts can't catch falling girls and they don't ladle on so much syrupy cologne that it sets fire to your eyes and nose. And last I heard, Dad wasn't dead, just gone.

I leap out of his arms and sneeze violently into my hands. I'm woozy from my almost fall, the heady cologne, and the obvious—him. Do not make eye contact! I frantically scan the pebbled parking lot for a garbage can to vomit in.

I feel Dad's smile before I see it.

"Sidonia."

He breathes my name like a prayer. I make the mistake of looking up at the skyscraper that is my Dad. He's so handsome, it can make you dizzy: rich brown eyes, dark against the cream of his skin, his nose perfectly broad and his lips just a little too full and pretty to look proper on a man. I shrink in his shadow, sway under his eyes. Then I remember that no one, only Mum, can get away with using the full, ridiculous version of my name.

"It's Syd now!" I punch out.

Flinch! Dad mumbles an apology. For a split second he looks woozy, but then he straightens up and smoothes everything over with a smile. His teeth are an eerie white: he's probably bleaching. How pathetic.

Just as I'm about to write him off, he morphs his features again—his eyes drip with sympathy, he shrinks until he's warm and vulnerable. I would be enveloped into his chest with a hug if I just said the word.

"I've missed you," he says instead, voice breaking.

Nice dart to the heart. It's official: I can no longer breathe. I blink back both sets of our tears and count stones in the gravel—smooth lake pebbles; if I swallow one, I'll never need to speak again.

Dad inhales and starts in on this long explanation about how he so wanted to see me before this. He had written, didn't I know? Except Mum must have intercepted the postcards, the letters, the emails, yadda, yadda, did I read them?

Could the Mum thing be true? It sort of sounded true: Crisp twenties and fifties from Dad would appear in a ripped-open envelope on my dresser. Why didn't they ever come with a card, a letter? Panic does the eensy-weensy spider thing up my bare arms. I cannot deal with this right now and Dad's voice is startling. I've stopped being used to it.

"Sidoni—, I mean, Syd?"

My eyes flick up to the right of Dad. There's a flash of red and, of course, she's there. Girl #2, fish eyes pressed through the window pane of a minivan, accusingly.

Quit looking at me! There's nothing I can do! Faceless Man didn't get me. My job's done, and maybe you'll notice, I'm busy with other things. The Absent Father showed.

I brush the invisible spiders off my arms. Where's Mum? Wasn't she just outside having a smoke?

Dad reaches for my scratched-up arm. "Siddie?"

I recoil in time. And Girl #2 is getting close; she's leap-frogged behind every car in the sparsely littered lot. Now she's leaning against a white Lexus, tapping her fingers on glass.

What are you waiting for?

"You shouldn't be here," I hiss to Dad. "Mum'll be back soon."

The mention of Mum shakes him for a moment. Dad licks his lips nervously.

"If your mother comes, then I will talk to her. What I'm most concerned about is you. I miss you. I miss . . . our talks."

Sounds heartfelt, Dad. Okay, you want to talk,

what should we talk about? That I beat Faceless Man?
Did you know? I went *wham-wham-wham* on his
head with a rough-ended rock! Alright, just one
wham—I let gravity do most of the damage, one drop
and maybe his skull split like a watermelon. Well, not
exactly—but he was *down* and I did it all by myself!
Very Big Girl. Very Good Big Girl.

And because I am Very Good Big Girl, I didn't just
leave him there. I waved my palm in front of his nostrils to make sure he was still breathing and I felt the
big artery in his neck for a pulse. No, for all my frantic rambling, I think I've known in my mind the whole
time I didn't *kill* him with that rock. I mean, he wasn't
dead when I left him, Dad. I just made him think twice
about scaring girls—a "you can get Syd once, but not
twice" kind of thing. They're going to have to make
up a distance for the record I set tearing out of those
woods—running from him.

And I wasn't quite alone either. See, Dad, Girl #2
helped me out. You probably don't know who I'm
talking about since you moved before . . . before. Let's
say she's not exactly of this world. And guess what?
She's running back and forth behind you right now,
trying to get my attention, trying to make me do something crazy. Shhh . . . she's not really . . .

And don't look at me like that! This is all absolutely
true! I swear it on this slippery red ruby heart that I'm
wearing on the outside of this flimsy dress, my heart
that beats louder and wilder than anyone else's. I

know you can hear it, Dad. Except, okay, yours must be beating pretty loud now, too.

Oh, and speaking of beating hearts, there's also this guy I like and now I can say his name instead of the stupid nickname my best friend picked for him and he's pretty cool, but my best friend, who isn't my best friend anymore because I betrayed her, will hate me even more for liking a guy she thinks she likes but has never even talked to. Because she doesn't know that I talked to him first. I can't win, can I?

And while we're still talking, did you know that since you've left, Mum is even more addicted to ciga-rettes and sad movies than ever before. I've had to give up watching TV at night completely because she'll be sitting by the patio door, cigarette in one hand, remote control in the other, smoking and sniffling away, so thanks for that, Dad.

Oh, yeah. One more thing: Don't tell me anything about your life. Don't tell me about the beautiful, stu-pid house you live in now or about your beautiful (or even ugly) new girlfriend or the trips you go on, trav-elling to tropical places where the sun always shines. Don't tell me any of that because I'll probably toss up my single morning muffin all over the pebbles in this parking lot.

Blood pounds through my eyes.

I'm sure I didn't say any of this aloud but Dad is looking at me like I'm a bomb ready to go off. In my mind I already did. Maybe he's realized I'm all grown up. After all, Mum made me wear pumps and I'm in this heinous grown-up dress, looking at him like I've got his number.

Except, he's looking behind me.

"Are you stalking us, Roy?" intones Mum from over my shoulder. Her face has hardened into tough scorned-woman mode: lashes stroked to kill, her geisha mask glued in place with hate and smouldering nicotine. She grabs my upper arm in a pincer grip.

"If this is what I'm forced to do," replies the Ice Prince.

I brace myself, waiting for Mum to blow. I shrink until I'm eight, caught in yet another parental argument; my feet swim in my grown-up shoes, the hem of my dress hits the gravel, Mum's grip on my arm tightens.

"Poor you," Mum shoots back.

Then it's rolling eyes and Dad saying "Clare, you're so predictable."

Then Mum's chiding about how, once again, Dad's proving how erratic and narcissistic he is, while she shakes my upper arm like a rag and hey—across the way! A red-haired girl dashes from behind a white minivan and dodges four lanes of traffic on the street. She halts at a bus stop, looking expectantly to the left. She's joined by other real people who are all looking left, waiting.

I shake off Mum's grip.

"I have to go pee," I mutter. I duck around the

corner, and across the path to the church's front entrance. My parents stop yelling for about two seconds—probably to make sure I didn't take off— that'll make them look back. But they're back at bitching at each other, which is good timing for me. The bus is in sight and I sprint across the church lawn, my wounded toe jamming into the front of my shoe as I run. The bus skids to a halt, and all the people waiting, including Girl #2, start to get on.

Now if I was just your average girl, the bus would take off even before I hit the street. Except I'm Syd Johansen, Etobicoke midget record holder for the 1,500 metre, and cross-country champ, and it's only about 150 metres from where I am to the bus stop. Easy.

I dodge traffic like a frenzied squirrel, wave my clutch purse at the driver once I hit the yellow line and run up the rubber steps. Sure, I'm pouring sweat in my silk dress but my breath is absolutely even.

Thank God for slimy bridesmaid purses, otherwise I wouldn't have had bus fare.

"Runaway bridesmaid?" The bus driver gives me a goalie grin—he's missing his two front teeth.

Since when do bus drivers actually talk to passengers on the Toronto bus? And since when do passengers actually look other passengers in the eye, never mind stare at their ugly dresses? I paste on a fake cheer. It's like everyone in the bus has decided that I'm their entertainment for the moment. Some are smiling, some are just staring blankly. Didn't you read the handbook?! No eye contact! Look away!

Of course, Girl #2 isn't among the passengers. Not that I expected she would be. I know where she's heading anyway.

Through the smeared window, I see my parents go by, stranded on the church lawn, mute and helpless. Mum gestures her arm toward the bus, turning to yell at Dad, probably blaming him for the whole episode. Dad heads back to the parking lot, maybe toward his car. Do not follow me! Luckily, Mum's right on his tail, she'll hold him up. Good—no one will follow me, no one will stop me.

#19
follow the girl

So here I am making my big breakaway on Toronto transit—woo hoo!—on a city bus that farts diesel dust and slides to a standstill every two minutes as it chugs down Eglinton Avenue. The only good news is we just passed the clump of forest that marks Kipling Avenue. It's not too much further.

What's on my mind is: if he did die, exactly how long does it take before a body starts to decompose? Because the high noon sun warms my neck and I'm thinking of Faceless Man's body cooking under it.

I gnaw at my thumbnail. Three more stops. Maybe if I stand, the driver will decide to go faster than his diesel crawl. Maybe Mum and Dad are trailing me in their cars right now and will fight over whose back seat they'll jam me into while they blame each other for my "running away." Maybe a dog will grab Faceless Man's shoe and bring it back to his owner, who will follow him back to the body in the Hornet's Nest.

Yeah, much better to stand. I wrap a sweaty palm

on a greasy bus pole and rise. My big toe shrieks in pain. The bus window frames the six whirling circles of concrete overpasses just up ahead. There's my stop.

"You sure you want to get off here?" the bus driver asks, concerned.

Clearly he doesn't know the neighbourhood. Does he think I'm going to throw myself into traffic? I can see the headline: Bridesmaid forced to wear peach, becomes suicidal!

I toss him a blank look as I disembark (which maybe wasn't nice, but made me forget what I was about to do), rip off my shoes (eww, the right toe is stained red), hike up my dress, and sprint barefoot across seven lanes of fresh asphalt. Good thing it isn't rush hour; everyone must still be at the mall.

I continue my run along the ripped-up bike path where the spongy grass soothes my arches. Running is good. The warmth in the wind buffets my cheeks; only the odd stone scrapes my heel. I feel almost normal, like I could forget anything. I turn to the left and duck under a canopy of green to my ravine.

I haven't been on this path since that October day; it figures Girl #2 would lead me to the grove where I first saw her drawing circles in the air with her foot. I brace myself to see her perched in a tree, but she isn't there.

A wind flattens my dress against my skin. There's a dirt stain on the skirt; maybe I should have gone home to change.

"Syd?"

It's a girl's voice; goosebumps break out over my skin.

Forget it! Girl #2 can't talk. At least she hasn't yet.

"*Syd*!" yells the voice. It's coming from behind me and the girl speaking is pissed off. It's Alicia—surly Alicia posturing behind the chain-link fence that separates the bike path from the concrete viaduct that runs under the Eglinton Bridge. She's hanging beside our second sacred tree, the Soul Tree, which is essentially a bush that pushed its way up through a crack in the concrete and sprouts purple flowers every spring. She's hanging with the skank named Melissa, who is squatting, unattractively I might add, by the Soul Tree and—get this—they're smoking. Future track stars—whatever.

Alicia is momentarily dazzled by the azure beading of my dress. I look down. Okay, maybe it's the smears of dirt on my silk skirt and my muddy and blood-encrusted big toe that's making her do the "sour lemon" face. I guess I would be gawking if I saw me like this too.

"Wedding rehearsal, remember?" I say, half-apologetically.

Sympathy flashes across Alicia's face, but only for a moment. Then it goes hard again.

Melissa snorts, "Nice dress," then digs into chewing the skin off her fingers through a hyena grin.

"Nice cigarettes." I point to her pack of smokes.

She laughs me off. I curse myself for saying something so lame. I should have said, Maybe you'll suck back a thousand cigarettes until you get cancer.

"So," Alicia juts out her hip like she's some tough mama, except her voice cracks with emotion, "I heard you and R.S. hooked up last night."

And there it is. Sure, if a five-minute conversation qualifies as getting lucky.

"We talked."

"Uh-*huh*," Alicia says.

Like I have to deal with *this* right now. Would you like a taste of my day? I want to scream at her! But I can't scream.

Melissa breaks a green twig off the Soul Tree and starts ripping it to shreds as her cigarette droops from her lips. Of course, *she* would be the lying snake in tight jeans. Of course, she would destroy the only piece of beauty along a stretch of dirty concrete. And along with it, any friendships she happens across.

Alicia continues, "I mean, if you had something going with him, that's fine, but don't try to pretend that you'd really like to see him with me, when all the while you're lying to my face, you, you . . ."

She stops short of using the B-word, I'll give her that. And she's doesn't like tearing into me. Big doll tears drip down her cheeks. I hold my own back.

Meanwhile, Melissa's finished shredding her branch and is trying to stub her cigarette on the concrete. No luck, instead it rolls down the concrete wall and falls into the creek.

"Let's leave Miss Bridesmaid," Melissa yawns. But Alicia is glued to the pavement.

"I can't believe you'd do this to me," Alicia blubbers, shaking. "But maybe I should have known, after what you did with Matt." Then she adds, so mouse-quiet I can barely make out her words over the frothy water: "I can't believe you're such a . . . a . . . slut."

A Molotov cocktail of anger threatens to burn up my insides. Yeah, that's me—a slut who happens to be a virgin. Explain to me how that works?

There goes my last friend in the real world. I turn my back on both of them—the ex-friend and her new skank pal—showing them the knives they've dug in. I leave them behind as I sprint on sponge grass until I hit the Hornet's Nest. I'll cry later. Right now I've got more important things to do.

#20
the hornet's nest

I arrive at the end of the forest, my forest.

From here I can see its sparse trees jutting out of the ground like old yellowed bones. There are only a few patches of green in the cluster of bare branches. It's hard to believe I ran in there thinking I'd have cover. My heart flip-flops up into my mouth as I survey the scene: It looks so *normal*. There's no telltale flap of yellow police tape, which has me both relieved and, for some reason, worried.

I scope out the parkette on the other side of the toboggan hill: the swings are still rendered useless, wrapped around the top bar, but there's a toddler and an older girl playing on the freshly painted monkey bars. A white-haired man is picking up what his tail-wagging golden retriever left in the grass with a plastic bag. There's no one else.

Which is a good sign, right? There wouldn't be families playing around here if the police had discovered his body. Or maybe they just haven't found him yet.

A series of images flood my mind, headlines that read "Papergirl slays stalker" above my secret tagline, "Avoids becoming Girl #3." I savour the swell of pride that follows along with the flurry of front-page photos: a close-up of my grin as the mayor hands me a key to the city at Nathan Phillips Square, television footage of a forgiving Alicia jumping up and down like a spastic freak in the front row, my mother radiant with pride, so proud of her daughter she's decided to leave the house other than for work, and wear colour—red for victory. Then there's Dad behind Mum, not touching but sort of close, suddenly moving to the front of the crowd with a wave and a warm smile that says "I miss you, too." And finally, Ian a.k.a. R.S., pointing out to his buddies that he knew all along I was cool.

But wait a minute, at the very back of the crowd is Matt. He doesn't belong in my fantasy, wearing that slinky grin of his that now completely repulses. I have the cheering crowd swallow him up, but even thinking about him leaves bile in my mouth. What am I doing here? What if Faceless Man is up and around and knew I'd come back to the scene of the crime? Can I just turn around and go back home, flip on the TV, and watch music videos all day? Can I turn back time and make sure Girl #1 makes it to her flute lesson and Girl #2 never has to warn me? I don't need to be a hero. I don't even need to know what happened.

No, this has to be done. I plunge into the forest,

eyes flitting here and there, on hyper-alert.

It's as if the woods are lit from the inside, the afternoon sun is that bright. Despite a few shadows lying here and there between the bare branches of trees and in dim-lit corners, there's serenity and a beauty to this place right now that's out of place, especially considering that I'm looking for the body of a man.

I take three baby steps, then pause, listen. I hear nothing (aside from the amplified pounding of my heart), so I continue. A stray branch stabs me in the left arch. I swear and hop on my previously wounded foot. I catch the edge of my dress on another skeleton tree and it pulls a raised line across the silk, but I can't worry about my dress. I'm hunting.

I crouch and extend my left hand to touch the outer wall of the Hornet's Nest, feel a small stab of pain, and immediately retract it. A droplet of blood forms on my fingertip. I don't think I've explained the Hornet's Nest properly, have I? It's a clearing in the bush, great for fort-making and certain covert teenage activities that rely on cover. That is, if you can get past the thick brambles full of thorns that encircle it.

I make like a cat on the hunt and crouch-step around the nest; one more step and Faceless Man should be lying in front of me. I muse about turning back, but I need to know. I need to know I'm not crazy. I need to believe in myself.

I step out from the Nest's shadow to stand in the exact spot where less than three hours ago a man who had only just grown eyes lay bleeding, possibly to death.

But there is no body, only a dapple of crisp autumn leaves that survived the winter snow and a thin breeze that ruffles a leaf.

I stand incredulous, then frantic. This can't be! I retrace my steps and find my tree. I place a bruised hand on the rough trunk. Thank God, the tree is real. I dig my fingers into its thick bark until it tears a layer off my fingertips. He should be lying right here, between the tree and the mouth of the Nest! But there's nothing here!

Am I crazy? Did this whole incident happen at all: the warning, the white car, the Faceless Man, the blood?

I frantically scan the ground for the rock that dealt the blow. Yes, if I find the rock, I will know it really happened. I grab all the loose rocks in my vicinity, overgrown boulders, small stones. I weigh them in my hands and drop each one with a crack. None of them feel right.

Feel the scratches on your face, the tear on your leg—of course, this happened!

Then I should find a puddle of blood at least the size of a cantaloupe at my feet. What did he do: Scoop it into a plastic bag and carry it away? The vein in my temple throbs. The throbbing travels to the edge of my eye and vibrates my vision, and suddenly I'm falling.

The leaves crackle under my folded knees. That's weird—the leaves look fresh, not like the black soggy leaves that emerge after a long winter. These leaves look crisp, like they just fell from a red maple in October, which would be perfectly normal if it wasn't the end of March.

I crawl forward and poke at the pile. The leaves crackle. I push more aside with both hands now, sift and lift in layers and until underneath I can feel slippery wetness. I pick up a single wet leaf and rub it between my fingers—dark red forms on the fingertips.

I brush a thick mound of leaves away and uncover the outline of a thought bubble, hidden.

Relief, like warm water, trickles down my spine. So now I know he was real. Then the relief turns to panic and guts me: He got away.

I dig my fingers into my face.

Not only did he get away, he cleaned up after himself as if none of it had happened. This is a game to him and I don't want to play any more.

I clamp my dirty hands over my mouth and try to strangle the scream in my throat—no dice. I scream like *I'm* being pummelled with a rock. I scream until my throat turns inside out: I *hate* that Alicia now thinks I'm some two-faced slut even though I'd stick pins in my eyes before I'd hurt her. I *hate* how my Mum cares so much about Dad. I hate that he left us. But what I really, really *hate* is that I'm so afraid, that I have all these stories about Girl #1 and I see Girl #2 in my head. And they won't go away until it's over. And it's not over.

When I'm done, I'm a raw wound—spent, crashed on my back in the fallen leaves, eyes filled with an empty sky.

A bell jingles near my head. I jolt upright. The golden retriever from the park sniffs a trail of concern toward me. My guardian. Soft eyes, gentle wag. I manage one stroke of his face when his white-haired owner barks a "Hunter! Come!" and my only friend high-tails it out of the forest and up the hill. His owner gives me a parting glare. Beyond him, through the trees, I see the monkey bars have also been vacated.

I've cleared the park. I might as well have screamed, "Fire!"

A giggle escapes—I can't help myself. I lie back, toss my head to and fro in the leaves. The leaves crackle and dry ones break into bits and lodge themselves in my spiky hair. I feel like shrieking in a crazed glee, it feels so good. I sit up. A tear of surprise tries to escape down my cheek, but I staunch it right away with the blunt palm of my right hand. No way. No tears. It is really beautiful and serene in these woods. There's another lilting breeze and the faintest aroma of rich earth, a harbinger of spring. I'm shaking, but now it's good. It's relief that I didn't kill anybody. And that I got away from somebody who probably would have killed me.

And while I'm sitting there, shaking in the leaves,

that's when I see her, sitting on a stone not more than
two metres away—so close. She's all angles: toes
pointed inward, elbows on thin knees, red hair hanging past her pointed chin. But it's the familiar leaf-
green eyes, luminous and transparent, that pin me to
the core: Girl #2.

Her gaze drinks me in. I'm paralyzed. She acknowledges me with a nod for the first time today. Then, still
pinning me with those eyes, she stands, turning her
back, and walking down the dirt path to the ravine.
You'd never guess she was a ghost. She walks like a
normal person would walk and stops just once where
the forest gives way to muddy grass, to check on me.
She resumes her walk, and I follow her into the gold
amber of an afternoon sun.

#21
girl #3

Mum never said anything about not following ghosts.

Never talk to strangers, Syd. Don't eat yellow snow! Wash your hands after you ride the subway.

Nope, nothing about not following ghosts in a ravine.

But Girl #2's ghost isn't scary. In fact there's something beautiful, ethereal, about her, like she's made of paint strokes brushed onto air. As I follow her across the muddy plains of the ravine, there's a lilt of hope in my step: Who else do I know who could possibly understand a fraction of what I've been through today? I have to follow her lead because she's the only one who could understand.

As it turns out, keeping up with her is not that easy. She may be made of paint strokes, but Girl #2 is deceptively fast. And I don't feel like I'm gaining any ground, mud squishing up through my toes. The bottom of my dress is now coffee-brown.

"Ally-Maude is going to be furious!" I hear my Mum rage.

When I look up again, out of breath, Girl #2 has already popped up by the creek. She seamlessly flows down the short slope to the creek, and floats up the opposite bank where old oak trees weave a thick canopy across the sky. Her figure flits through the gnarled trunks like dapples of light. I run to keep up.

When I arrive at the place where she crossed the creek, I see no path of riverbed stones that she could have stepped on. The water is thick and frothy, a swollen torrent courtesy of spring runoff—that's what you get for following a ghost. A shiver runs up my neck and I sprint to a concrete foot bridge ahead, cross it and follow her path under the wide oaks. I can see where termites have eaten into them and spat out their orange insides.

I never travel on this side of the creek—there's no asphalt, not even a dirt path to weave around the fat trunks. Even when Alicia and I go to the Soul Tree, we stick to the bike paths on the safe side until we're forced to pop over the concrete viaduct.

I delicately tiptoe over fallen branches and sharp twigs. Dense bush climbs the curve to the bungalows above and, even without their leaves, the oaks throw dark shadows. I duck the odd hanging branch, but a stray one catches my right cheek and scrapes skin. My lungs hurt from my sprint and now I've completely lost sight of her. I know she's heading north because that's the only direction I can go and she wants to show me something, right? Why else would she have me follow her? Or am I following her because I need her to have to tell me something?

Or maybe it's none of these things and Girl #2 doesn't even exist. I'm following air. I've trusted my gut and been wrong before. And maybe I've invented her because she seems so lost, like I am. Still, I keep moving.

I'm panting as I run. I trip over a tree root. I stumble as I recover, catching the thorns of a bush on my right temple. When I emerge, panting and delirious, soles slippery with mud, Girl #2 is calmly standing on the Eglinton viaduct, her toes pointing down the angled "V" of the concrete to the swollen drizzle below, those leaf-green eyes so soft.

The serenity doesn't last. Once my dirty foot is scraped by pavement, she turns and continues her walk to nowhere, her spine forming a perfect vertical line despite the steep angle of the wall she walks on, past the Soul Tree where Alicia and Melissa were smoking their cheap cigarettes. They're gone, but the stink of menthol and nicotine turns my empty stomach as I walk past, my bare feet gripping the sloped concrete.

Girl #2 isn't interested in the Soul Tree. She ducks into darkness under the Eglinton Avenue Bridge, delicately sidestepping crude spray jobs of genitals and profanity. She ignores the empty beer bottles lining the horizontal shelf at the top and continues on until she pops into the sunlight again past Eglinton. This March sun has magically turned the concrete into the colour of warm sand.

The butterflies take flight in my belly as I follow. Like the path, I've never been on the other side of the bridge before. I tuck my chin down so my head won't hit the concrete rafters blackened with diesel dust and earth, each low beam acting like a divider that creates rooms on the top shelf under the bridge. I focus on the rubber soles of Girl #2's ballet slippers as she places one foot precisely in front of the other. Out of the corner of my eye I see each rafter room occupied by a different mocking face: a drunken rummy, a stoned teen, a pouting Japanime girl, all looking at me. Of course, they aren't real—it's just graffiti (the smoking purple dinosaur on the end gives it away).

I emerge unscathed on the north side of the bridge. Over here, solid concrete like angled prison walls stretches up the hill to the tenement towers, the high-ways clashing in the sky like a blackjack wheel with cars spinning in all directions, across the city, to the lake, past the airport. The sound of highway traffic is a constant backdrop.

Girl #2 keeps her measured walk on the angled walls, curving upward to avoid one of the open-mouthed sewers that jut out of the concrete. As I follow her climb, I peer down to see its grated gate dripping with rotting newspapers and garbage. The stench of decomposing fruit tickles my nose hairs. I pinch my nostrils and breathe through my mouth. I watch this stretch of sewer water feed directly in the creek to the south and try not of think of summers past wading in that water, farther up where it's a real creek, with my Dad, looking for crayfish.

Then Girl #2 comes to what appears to be her final destination. She passes a spindly tree and sits down beside it. She manages a smile, and though it's slight, I feel like she's given me her warmest welcome.

The tree she sits by isn't pretty like the Soul Tree. It's the definition of ugly: a porcupine bush that farted its way out of a crack in the concrete. Is this dead twisted tree what she wanted to show me? It can't be. She doesn't give me any clue sitting there, quiet, leaf-green eyes expectant, the wind catching vibrant strands of her red hair. She looks down beside her, like she wants me to sit there.

I feel a swell of pride that I can barely contain: of all the other girls in the world, Girl #2 has chosen me, not only to appear before, but to sit with! Still, sitting right beside her is unthinkable. Too weird. I sit and immediately feel the stubble from the concrete through my dress. I might as well be naked.

I'm sitting next to a ghost. Just in case, I leave her a respectful bubble of space.

We say nothing. In the silence, I pick at a loose cuticle on my left thumb. I hear my mother's chiding about unkempt hands in my head. I stop and pick up

a gnarled stick that fell from the Porcupine Tree, digging a thumbnail under the bark and flicking it off. In-
credibly, Girl #2 picks up a similar twig, or maybe it's
just the twirl of the tree in the—air. I'm trying so hard
not to look directly at her—afraid that she'll disappear, or afraid that she isn't really there and I'm really,
truly losing my mind.

There is so much I want to ask her, so much that
the sheer number of questions has created a log jam in
my throat. I know I absolutely don't want to ask her
about *it*, but going the small-talk route—talking
about, I don't know, what's your favourite band—
seems disrespectful in a completely opposite way. So I
wait for her to say something. But after—what—five,
ten, fifteen minutes of no words, just the whirl of cars
and the inevitable thud their tires make as they race
over the expandable metal joist of the bridge, I realize
she is calmly waiting for me to go first.

The stupidest, most obvious question springs from
my lips. "Is there something you want to tell me?"

Everyone knows (and everything on television and
in movies says) that ghosts come back only if they
have to tell you something really special, right? I mean,
they have access to all the secrets in the universe, and
they come back when they need to share one with
someone who's living. But what does this ghost have
to do with me? What could she have to say to me?
Wouldn't it make more sense for her to appear to the
man who killed her? She doesn't say anything, not a

word to help me out, but maybe—do ghosts have vocal chords?

After another twenty cars hit the metal joist on the Eglinton Bridge, I hear something. I look closer and see her lips are moving. I strain to listen and I hear them—Girl #2's faint words, like a bird's song lost in traffic:

My name is Rachel.

Of course, I know her name is Rachel. Everyone knows her name is Rachel, just like everyone knows that the name of her cat was Tripod because he only had three legs and that Rachel called him Captain Kitty when she was younger because of the one black patch circling his eye. That on The Day her mother knew something was wrong when she got home because Tripod was yowling a "Where's Rachel? Where's Rachel?" and by the time her father got home, her mother had already called the school and all of Rachel's closest friends then the police, and the awful thing is, according to the papers, she was still alive at that point.

I force my memory to fast-forward over these details, clamp my eyes shut on this unwanted recall. You don't need to know. You've probably heard a hundred stories like it in the news since then.

"Uh, I'm Sidonia," I say in return, my voice bouncing off the concrete walls, surprising myself with my own name. It's a grown-up name, and somehow, finally, it seems to fit.

That's a pretty name.

"I hate it," I blurt out.

Rachel gives the faintest hint of a nod, or maybe it was the wind blowing a few strands of her hair. I still can't bring myself to look directly at her.

We sit in more silence by the Porcupine Tree. It's weird, I know so many things about this person's life and yet what I know is nothing at all. What can we really talk about? I give up trying and look straight at her for the first time. She looks like a real person, not spectral at all; talking to her is perfectly reasonable.

"So, why are you here?" I ask hoarsely.

Not even the wind answers. Girl #2 is entranced by the blue-green drizzle that is what's left of the creek on the industrial side of the bridge as it slithers through its concrete vice and gushes into the sewer. I shift my weight and feel the fibres of silk catch and tear on the concrete—maybe going home to change would have been the right course of action. When Girl #2 still says nothing, I can't take it anymore.

"He got away, didn't he?" I croak. "I might as well not have come back."

Still no response. Maybe I'm misled by how real she looks. If someone walked by right now, would they see a girl in a torn peach dress sitting near an ugly tree talking to the air?

I keep yapping, all of it pouring out, like a dam has broken.

"Another guy I know got away with it ... my best

friend Alicia, she's a little naive and she went off with this guy, Matt, into the woods at this dance that she wasn't allowed to go to but lied to her parents about. So I had to protect her, right? I mean, she can't take care of herself. She wouldn't know a bad guy, a really bad guy, from a guy that was okay as long as he wore the right kind of shoes and was kind of cute, right? So I went into the ravine, I went into the forest because I heard giggling and I thought it was hers. But it was pitch dark, it was like walking into a pot of ink, until I saw this flash. Like a spark. They had started a fire. They. He. Matt, I guess. He's this guy ..."

A guy I liked, maybe, liked as much as I hated him, now that it's possible that no one's here to hear me say it.

It's like I'm sitting in an auditorium listening to myself recite a speech over the sound system: every "um" is amplified, every "I" is razor sharp; I cringe over every detail, but keep going.

"They were hidden under the lip of the Hornet's Nest. Matt. His buddy Cam and this girl ..."

In my mind's eye I see this giggling mass of dark curls reddened with the firelight. I *had* to go in and get Alicia. I already had a story in hand: My mum called. She says your dad's freaking out, wants to talk to you to make sure you're safe.

Then Matt popped up like one of those loose-limbed jack-in-the-boxes.

"Hey, it's Cherry. Cherry, Cherry," he cooed,

seductive. "Looking for your friend?" He grinned so wide it nearly split his face. "She's here with us," he said.

So I stepped into the nest. No surprise. He used the line to lure me in. But once I walked into his trap, I saw that the girl wasn't Alicia. She was some chick named Kiera who was so stoned or whatever, all she could do was giggle like a pull-string doll. But she was with Cam, and Matt, well, it looked like he was alone.

"Come sit a while . . ."

He patted earth; the coolness of it would seep through my pants. Yeah, I could sit for a bit. Why not? I had to admit, Matt was gorgeous, even if he did have a look like a shark about to bite.

Bottles clinked. Splashed liquid splattered mud. I shook my head furiously as a bottle came my way, kept my back ramrod straight.

Don't give anything away. Alicia's the one that likes Matt. He repulses you, remember?

Matt chuckled softly, his body as warm and as open as a kiss and he inched closer. If he touches me, I thought, I'll explode.

But maybe I wouldn't. I let my spine melt, just a little; let his warmness envelop me, felt his heat on my cheeks, painting my ear, my mouth, every solid part of me dissolving under his touch. Why not? I could just let it happen, have our lips meet, his moist and ruby, felt a hand reach up and curl fingers in my hair and hissed so only I could hear . . .

"See, it's cherry red." (Like he could see in the dark.) "Just like that girl that went missing; the one downtown." He leered: "Except I've found you."

Girl #2 is still listening. Am I still talking out loud? I drone on.

"Well, I might as well have been shot with ice bullets. I was paralyzed when he said that, and that's when he made his move. I mean, it's not like anything big happened—I'm a virgin—obviously. And I fought like a wildcat. I started flailing around, did some whirling kicks. I think I caught him in the knee 'cause it felt like a rock and it really hurt my big toe, tripping over drunk-and-stoned Kiera and Cam who were past the PG-13 stage, and Matt laughing in the background. I wasn't even there for a minute. And maybe I would've just been able to forget it—but, but . . ."

Then they found you again.

". . . then Matt started tailing me in the hallways, snickering. I'd duck into the washroom. Cut class. Then he'd call me . . . I don't even know how he got my cell number."

There were only three phone calls, technically, but that was enough. Two when I went home at lunchtime, which pissed me off mostly, but then one more at night when Mum wasn't back from work. That scared the crap out of me. The nights were growing darker, winter air was howling outside, and I would see faces in the patio doors.

Then, suddenly, they stopped. Got bored, I guess.

They moved on, forgot about me. I didn't forget. Especially since Melissa put the bug in Alicia's ear that I was with Matt and *with* him—a guy who was the favourite of all the neighbourhood mums who didn't want to believe he thought abducting girls was funny, or worse.

"Anyway, it doesn't matter anymore," I say aloud. I release the grip on my thighs, wipe the tears with the back of my hand. I realize I feel lighter; my shoulders relax.

Rachel stands.

Startled, I immediately jump up. She moves closer to me. This close-up, I see her skin is as solid as mine— so real—and our eyes lock. I read Girl #2's mind.

You haven't beaten Faceless Man.

I want to protest but something about the way she's looking at me freezes the words on my tongue.

He's healing now. The boulder didn't do anything. You know what will happen when he's better.

Don't tell me!

He'll be back on the road soon and he'll be working with his accomplice, the taxi driver. They've got other friends who helped with me, who didn't get caught, like the taxi driver. They'll keep playing their games unless you stop them.

Oh, God. I squirm under her glare. I wish I could run to my side of the bridge—the safe side, but she's not letting me go, not until she's done what she came here to do.

*There will be a Girl #3. . . . Not today but maybe
tomorrow or not, or maybe it will be next year even,
or the year after that or the year after that. And maybe
Faceless Man will be the one who does it or maybe it
will be someone else who does it. The only thing we
know—you, Sidonia, and I—is that today, it wasn't
you. But in a tomorrow it will be someone else. And
maybe she won't be as lucky.*

The enormity of this overwhelms me. I put my face
in my hands and bawl like I've never bawled before—
bawling over Girl #2, Girl #1, Faceless Man, Alicia,
Matt, Mum and Dad, these whole terrible two years.
My sobs drown out the thunder of traffic, the jets
flying overhead, the constant jarring of rubber tires
hitting the metal barrier.

Girl #2 doesn't comfort me. She stares past my
shoulder, into the algae-blue dribble of the creek. I
realize in between sobs that she's done what she
needed to do. And now she's leaving.

I watch as she continues her airless walk north—
she is as unaffected as I am devastated. Her spine is taut
as she curves uphill to bypass another sewer grate in the
viaduct wall, then she disappears entirely from view.

The flesh around my eyes is red and raw. I know
what I have to do but, strangely, I'm not as afraid as I
thought I'd be. It's like a bit of Rachel is left in a par-
ticle of air and she's saying: *You're ready. If someone
calls you a liar, if they try to twist your words, you
won't let them. Your truth will win.*

I heave myself to my feet, feeling unspeakably heavy and tired. I have to answer my mother's question honestly. No, not okay. I have to tell her about Faceless Man. I have to make sure they find him, that they stop him. If Mum doubts me for a second, I'll march us both down to the police station. And if they won't listen to me, I'll have to dig and scratch and find someone else. I will have to scream until they listen. I will paint it in a blood-red scrawl a metre high on the backs of buildings, in the schoolyard, in the playground, on the ravine pathway if I have to.

Anything to make sure there won't be a Girl #3.

After

#22
after

This summer's going to be a scorcher. The mid-morning sun glows a molten orange over the equally orange track at Centennial Park. It's June 1 and I'm the only one out of eight antsy competitors who still has her track suit on.

"Keep your nylon suit on until the official comes up with his gun!" bellowed Coach Bremner as we were warming up, his face turning as red as his angry unibrow. "I don't care if you're sweating buckets. You have to keep your limbs warm."

Yeah, well, I'm so warm standing on the grassy sidelines, I feel like one of those roasted chickens you get in a foil-lined paper bag at the grocery store—all slimy skin and nervous because I'm going to get eaten. Though the main difference is a chicken is already dead, I guess, and I'm alive and freaking out on the inside.

I cast a sidelong glance at the other seven girls who soon will be lining up with me behind the white line.

I envy their naked limbs courtesy of spandex shorts and sports bra tanks. They may be cooler, but I bet their hearts are thumping as loud as mine.

I gotta keep moving! I alternate jumping jacks with knee raises with frantically noshing on a hangnail. This race is momentous: it's the Ontario's—the provincials—and I've made the final for the 800 metres.

I'm going to barf. I'm going to barf up my single-egg-on-toast breakfast all over the neon orange track.

No, you're not.

But I am hot. Screw you, coach. I unzip and take off my jacket, revealing the worn brown tank top of Parkside C.I. that gives my skin a lovely toilet paper tone. Have I mentioned brown is not my colour? Still, the air hits my sweat-drenched arms and for a glorious few minutes, I feel the sweet cool of a summertime breeze drying all the nervous water droplets from my skin. I drag my palm across the back of my neck and wipe a thick film of sweat away.

Mum surprised me by insisting not only on coming to the meet but also driving me here—I don't dare look up to the south part of the grandstand where she's positioned herself right across from the finish line, beside the cheese-and-nacho stand. If I look over and see her chowing down on a dish of radioactive cheese, then I'll know I'll have to order the exorcism.

Poor Mum—first Dad leaves and now all this stuff I dumped on her. Needless to say, she's had plenty to

be freaked out about this past year—I can't believe a
whole year has gone by. So much has changed (Ian)
and some things haven't changed enough (Dad's not
coming back, but at least Mum and I talk about him
and I can call him and he can call me, which isn't that
much of an improvement, but it's a start, I guess.)
Anyway.... It's also been a year and two months since
that day in the ravine.

One of those sneaky breezes catches a fringe of my
still-growing hair and stabs it in my eyes, making them
tear up.

*You cannot think about it. You have a race to run,
a major race.*

Easier to say than do: There are reminders of my
fourteen-month ordeal hidden like rotten Easter eggs
all over this stadium.

When I lined up for my first heat, I caught the
attention of two girls from a school up north. One had
this goofy golf-ball stare while her friend narrowed
her raccoon eyes while giving me a "what's so special,
I could take her" look. I tried to shake their gazes that
lingered on my body too long. I wish I could say that
they were whispering about how last week I smashed
the Toronto record in the 800 metre (this time for junior girls—I'm beyond midget), but I know better. I'm
that girl they whisper, chat, and text about in hallways, on cellphones, on websites—the girl who was
almost abducted but lived to tell.

A pimply-faced official ambles over to our group

of finalists. He gestures with his whistle for us to follow him to the line.

It's showtime.

Great—I have to pee. In fact, every cell of my body wants to urinate, whether it can release water or not. This happens before every race. And the old Syd would have stood rigid, fearful that any motion would have set off the pee factor. But the new Syd ignores it, glowers at the track. Beside me, a blonde girl dressed in the red and white of Ian's school laughs nervously.

"It's about time," she says aloud, nodding her head to the official so her ponytail shakes. She looks over at me and smiles nervously, in the "everything's going to be alright" kind of way that some girls do before a competition, so maybe you'll be nice and not want to smoke their butt. I decide to ease her nerves with a brief smile. I can afford it.

Pimply-Faced Guy waves his bony white arms at our group. All of us follow with feigned boredom. I know if I look ahead and to my left, I'll see Ian warming up in a circle of his own. I've told him not to talk to me before a race—I can't take it. So far he's complied, but I don't dare look up: One gaze will distract me entirely. Reduce me to a pile of mush when I need to focus. I think of him anyway; his final is right after mine.

He's thinking of me, too. Even though I'm looking at my spikes marching in the grass, I can feel the heat from his look as he appraises me, remember the stretch of his lips under my fingertips last night, his words ("It will be a cakewalk for you") in our pre-race talk. I look over quickly, and catch the sly turn of his lips as he stretches beside the pole-vault pit. He knows I'm sneaking a peek. I can't think of him, or our two months of going out (though we've been friends for seven since his old girlfriend dumped him for a university guy). If I do, my body will burst into flames.

I shake my head to clear it and fix my gaze out in front of me. Past the track gates, in the parking lot I spy the telltale roof light of a police cruiser. My body goes on semi-alert. A young, white cop in short sleeves leans one beefy arm against the open driver's door. He's chatting casually to an older, dignified-looking black man. This guy isn't dressed in uniform but you can tell from the relaxed stance of his body that the two men know each other.

I squint into the sun. Could it be Clarkie?

"Let me get this straight: you're reporting an assault and your daughter is the perpetrator?"

That was 911 operator's response after Mum called—big mistake. For the operator, that is. See, I got home from my tête-à-tête with Girl #2, soul afire with purpose, only to find the house empty. Again. I sat on the porch for Mum until the concrete bled through silk and skin. But it was okay. I was no longer afraid of the repercussions. I had a new purpose, which Mum apparently read in my eyes once she skidded the Beamer into the driveway.

I have to tell you something.

"Scream what you mean" and "Action now!" These were Mum's new mottos after The Talk. After I spilled the disjointed mass and Mum made her aborted police operator call, Mum then called Dad and screamed. She called Gord-O at *The Carrier* and screamed some more. She packed me up and drove me to the Bloor Street police station, suddenly paranoid that Faceless-Now-with-a-Face Man might come and slaughter us in our beds (her words, not mine).

At the station, I expected Mum to mow through all the info officers all framed in neat glass and steel booths like some carnival game. Luckily, we got a man with quiet eyes who assured us that a uniform would be dispatched to the scene to see if the man was still there. (Duh—no!) And I could talk to a detective from the Sexual Assault and Child Abuse Section. Excuse me? Child abuse? I felt like crawling under one of the fake potted ferns that fanned the front windows. I muttered-prayed-begged Mum for us to please, please go home.

At least I got out of the wedding. I can't help but split a grin as I rotate my ankles, hands on hips. Mum did embellish to A-M, saying that I was attacked while wearing the dress, which explained its, er, sorry state. When A-M pressed for details, Mum shamed her into silence. Imagine—of all people, Mum turned out to be my alibi out of an important family function. This is huge for a woman who counts appearances above all else. She decided to protect me.

And my Booger Face usher had to walk the aisle solo. Ha!

Some irritable chick from Ian's school catcalls me from the sidelines: "Hey, Laughing Girl. Move your butt."

Whoops! All the other girls are strutting toward the start line. I jog to catch up.

Was I really giggling out loud? I picture a miserable Darek in his snotty rental suit having only his own gangly hands to hold on to at the altar. Oh yeah, I was definitely laughing.

As I jog, I'm also jogging home from the ravine and Girl #2, a shoe in each fist. The enormity of my decision to tell hits me when I get home. I pound up the stairs and puke in the toilet.

When I finally tell Mum, the words that have piled up in my throat spill out all over the floor. I watch her already pale face drain of more colour. Her eyes turn a weird pink-purple. Veins I never noticed pulsate in her temples and throat.

Faceless Man, a.k.a. Jason Lamont Reade, pushed her over the edge; he pushed me over the edge. Maybe in a weird, kind of sick way, I'm glad he did. What doesn't kill us makes us stronger, and all that, right?

I catch up with the other girls at the starting line and sneak a look behind to where Clarke the detective (or whoever this guy is) is behind a long strip of hedge, out of view. I'm surprised to feel disappointed. I could have sworn it looked like Clarke, Detective

Alistair Clarke from SACA (the acronym was more palatable). This guy was even wearing the same type of clothes Clarke would wear: loose tailored slacks and a nice short-sleeved button shirt that wasn't too casual or too formal. Everything about him was just right. Like the papers (I was even interviewed by one of the big-time papers), like the other runners who are looking at me just so, he knows all the details.

But what is he doing here? Why would he come see you run? How would he know that you were even running in these finals? The last time you talked to him was, like, two months ago.

Yeah, right near the anniversary, when he had news.

We've reached the white of the starting line: Everything starts and ends here. My legs twitch like horses ready to bolt. Pimply-Faced Guy directs us to our staggering position. I finally take time to scope out my competition.

All the girls are taller than me—no surprise there. The fiercest one has a near shaved head and her right ear is a mass of silver rings. She gets lane one, my favourite. At least I got lane two. I can see everyone else ahead of me except for the snorting bull, Multi-Earringed Girl behind me.

Tadpoles make somersaults in my belly.

Pimply-Faced Guy pulls out a starter pistol from his track suit pocket and suddenly becomes Race Starter Man. The pistol transforms him as he holds one thin freckled arm aloft and thunders with new authority:

"*Runners*, take your mark!"

I lunge for the white line, making sure there's no sliver of orange between it and my shoe. Pre-Faceless Man, I would have hung back until other runners had moved up to the line. Still, the tadpoles in my belly are now frogs and have graduated to double hand flips and gastro-diving: How the heck did I let Bremner convince me to run in the 800 metres? I hate the 800 metres! You have to sprint until your heart explodes for the first lap then you have to do it again! Bremner thought it would be good to "challenge me." (Yeah, don't think I've been challenged enough this past while.) But I guess he must be right because I'm here. And I guess I should be grateful: Bremner doesn't treat me any differently. In fact, I'd say he went out of his way to pretend like he didn't know every inch of my ordeal, like everybody else in my neighbourhood, in the city.

Once I'm hunched over the line, I decide to breathe. Alicia once told me that some fear is good for you. She said this a long time ago when we were still close. She hangs with Melissa now. She said the news of Faceless Man (I'd still rather call him that than his real name—weird, eh?) freaked her out, and maybe we weren't as close friends as we thought because how could I not confide in her? What she didn't mention was that Ian is the more likely reason that we don't talk anymore. Ian: There is nothing hidden in his kiss, only the surprise of it always being good. Okay, so it might not be so smart to give up your best friend for a guy, but a best friend stands by you through thick and thin, and forgives your stupid mistakes. And this guy feels good . . .

Concentrate!

"Get ready . . ." yells Pimply-Faced Guy.

I go rigid as I lean into my stance, my legs poised to spring and snap. I guess this is it.

Some fear is good, some fear is good, *some fear is good*, I chant silently, a bit hysterically.

The gun rings out, twice in rapid succession—false start. Multi-Earringed Girl is at fault and she halts her sprint after whipping by my stunned frame then sulks like a jaguar back to her starting position. Blond Ponytail in lane three rolls her eyes.

"She always does this," she mouths to me.

My concentration is blown. Now I have to get psyched again. I have to keep the fear at bay.

He'll be out when I'm eighteen.

Why the heck did I have to think about that *now*? Detective Clarke admitted as much in our living room in March as I sat, as always, on the couch with Mum who was chewing ferociously on nicotine gum, her swallows audible. At first my description of Faceless Man and the taxi driver accomplice had been put in the system and circulated. No matches found. Clarkie would talk to me in circles using terms that were alien and formal at the same time: "explicit invitation," "sexual touching." I'd mutter a "no...no," but I don't think he believed me so I stopped answering those questions. I'd dive into the deep pink shag of the living room carpet while my empty body sat rooted on the couch. Until he or Mum would change the subject, and I'd suss out the silence before returning to my skin.

How can you answer a question when you've never been given the proper words?

In the end, my half-remembered jumble of lines and circles turned out to be a bonafide licence plate number. Once I found that fact was solid, I grabbed it and hounded Clarkie every time he contacted us. Every time, we got the same spiel:

They had found the car but it was registered to some old guy in his fifties or something. He might have been Faceless Man's dad, but Clarkie wouldn't divulge anything like that to me and Mum. As for the man fitting my description—the flesh-and-blood description, not the faceless one—it was like he had evaporated with the last remnants of snotty snow. Probably went to Florida, went the joke, even though, by this point, spring had broken out in lush splendour.

It went like this for a while. When Clarkie came over to go over my story every time he thought he had a lead, I gave him the same story and he gave me the same—they were looking into it and all we could do was wait. I'd escape to the kitchen while my mother went all indignant. And Clarke would calm her down.

He's the only person we met in this process who has a mellowing influence on my mother. Everything about him was subdued and calm, from the way he moved to his formal, quiet voice that cradled me like a hammock in a sea breeze. Most importantly, he never questioned that it had happened, suggested I made it up out of thin air. In the kitchen alone, listening to their low voices, I would clench my fists until my nails dug into my palms, then study the raw red indents each nail had made in my flesh until he left.

Then magically, near the end of January, Faceless Man emerged from his hiding place up north or down south or wherever it was, and this time the police were there to catch him. It was the licence plate number that did it. Clarke had me pick him out from a group of photos. After I picked the right one, Clarke told me Faceless Man's real name, which resounded meaningless in my ears. I hardly even recognized the small squirrelly man they managed to photograph: I remembered him as bigger, more dangerous—less pathetic. But it was him, as sure as the chill that snaked down my spine when I laid eyes on him for the second time in my life. I did it. He was caught.

I felt great, that is until Clarkie started asking the whole "was there sexual touching or invitation to sexual touching" thing. That's the only way he could be charged—if I had been damaged. My mind went all Alice down the rabbit hole. I was ashamed to say there wasn't any touching: How screwed up is that? Maybe if there had been, he have gotten a longer sentence. Again—messing up thinking! I mewed the truth again—"no" and let a yawning silence grow between us.

After an eternity, Clarkie said he understood, said they had him with this other assault. The other girl was pressing charges and he was "cautiously optimistic" about a conviction. Then the Crown might decide to proceed with mine or that they might use my case in arguing for a longer sentence. I didn't get all of it, frankly. Detectives talk like lawyers who wish they could talk like normal humans.

What I did get was that my case would always be in the system, a permanent black mark against Faceless Man. What I got was that he got his hands on another girl, that he actually attempted something sexual. . . .

My blood boils. Nope, not going there. If you want to know the details of this, read the paper. But even then you won't know. You have to read the Internet postings and even there, weed through the crap, the bad spellings, the lies. Still, the thought of it makes me so mad I can barely hear Pimply-Faced Guy order us to our mark. Oh—wait. I'm running a race. Luckily, my body's working on instinct, and resumes its starting stance.

"Can you tag him?" I had asked Clarkie, fists shaking. Clarke pretended like he didn't know what I meant. "You know, like they do for animals before letting them loose in the wild." Brand him, track him, sew a GPS device under his skin.

Of course, these things would be illegal. Clarke told me not to worry, that Faceless Man is now their responsibility, theirs to worry about. Not mine.

He doesn't know it's my responsibility. Girl #2 told me as much, not that I've shared that with anyone. I don't want to appear too crazy.

"You've done everything you can."

That's what Mum said, before adding that she loved me, and did I know how proud she was of her brave daughter? I do, but I didn't say it. Keep her guessing.

Right now a stream of sweat curls around my eyebrow bone, dripping down into and stinging my eye.

The official calls out: "Get *set*!"

In case you're just tuning in, I'm the girl who lived to tell her story to the paper. I'm the girl who still has a voice, who still has breath in her lungs, whose blood is on fire. I'm the girl who told on Faceless Man. I set the dogs on the path. How could I possibly be afraid of anything?

Then, suddenly, the gun cracks and my body is running without thinking, the best way to run, the wind caressing my skin and cutting a tunnel around me. Out of the furthest corner of my eye, I see Ian watching me, that wry smile of his egging me on all the way down the track.

Oh, and this race? It's mine.